# THE RADICAL NOVEL RECONSIDERED

A series of paperback reissues of mid-twentieth-century
U.S. left-wing fiction, with new biographical and critical
introductions by contemporary scholars.

*Series Editor*
Alan Wald, University of Michigan

The People from Heaven

# The People from Heaven

JOHN SANFORD

Introduction by Alan Wald

University of Illinois Press
Urbana and Chicago

*This book is printed on acid-free paper.*

Library of Congress Cataloging-in-Publication Data

Sanford, John B., 1904–
The people from heaven / John Sanford ; introduction
by Alan Wald.
p.      cm. — (The Radical novel reconsidered)
Includes bibliographical references.
ISBN 0-252-06491-7 (pbk.)
I. Title. II. Series.
PS3537.A694P46      1995
813'.52—dc20                                      94-45900
                                                                CIP

To Nathanael West
1903–40

. . . And the others went running from house to house
and to the neighboring villages, with loud cries of
"Come! come to see the people from Heaven!"

—Christopher Columbus to
Luis de Santangel

# PREFACE

In 1936, when you first met her, Marguerite Roberts was a screenwriter for Paramount Pictures. Your second novel had recently been published, and Paramount had brought you to the West Coast in the belief that you might be of some use in the scenario department. The belief was ill founded. It took the studio a year to discover its error, but Marguerite—by then your wife and long since Maggie—had always known that you were on the wrong tack: your flair, she said, was for the making of books, and she was so certain of it that she volunteered to maintain you at that work on the earnings of her flourishing career. No marriage could have been more magical, though to your sorrow it lasted for only a half century. During that time, she enabled you to add eighteen books to the two written earlier, and it is solely to her, therefore, that you owe whatever you may have achieved.

*The People from Heaven* was written in 1942 and published in the following year. Long before that, Maggie had known of your extreme political views, and while she never interfered with your freedom to write as you chose, she *was* curious about how you'd come by those views. Yours had been a middle-class background, she said; you were a university man and a member of the Bar of the State of New York; you'd never worked for wages or walked a picket line; you'd never even been close to a mill or a mine or a pick and shovel. Instead, she said, you'd squandered four-month summers at the seashore and taken sabbaticals in London, Paris, and Madrid. Sabbaticals from what, John? From what year-round drudgery did you flee to the Riviera and Rome? Tell me, she said—how did one so privileged wind up on the Left, so very far from home?

You answered her thus: "I'm doing penance. Fifteen years ago, I was so vastly ignorant that I hadn't heard of Sacco and Vanzetti until the night of their execution. I don't know what I was up to during the seven years of their agony. All I can say is that they came into existence for me only when their existence ended, and my shame was so overwhelming that it sickened me. My emptiness was a sin, and I had to acknowledge it and atone for it, but I had to wait until I'd learned to write. I've learned enough to begin, and I begin with *The People from Heaven*."

"Never stop," she said. "Not till you die."

—J.S.

x

# INTRODUCTION

## Alan Wald

*The People from Heaven* is a 1943 novel by an unrepentant Jewish-American Marxist about anti-Black and anti–Native American racist culture in the North of the United States. The setting is Warrensburg, New York, then a small rural town in the Adirondack mountains where John Sanford vacationed in the summer of 1931 in the company of his personal and literary friend Nathanael West.[1] Except for a handful of dissenters and outcasts opposed to the local thug who runs the town, the subconscious life and daily values of most members of the fictional community are profoundly deformed by the culture and social system evolving from the violent conquest of the continent by Europeans that started in the seventeenth century.

Sanford's bitingly ironic title refers to his epigraph, which cites the reported cry of celebration of the native peoples of the Americas as they hailed the arrival of Columbus and the Europeans who would enslave them— "Come! come to see the people from Heaven!" The pattern of brutality enacted four hundred years earlier underlies the catastrophic events Sanford depicts in 1943: a propertied white man, Eli Bishop, rapes an itinerant Black woman, who is locally referred to as "America Smith," and then seeks to extend his reign of terror against a American Indian father and son, an independent-minded prostitute, and, finally, a Jewish refugee from czarist pogroms.

The advanced thinking underlying the symbolic action of the text is worth noting. Two decades before the writings of Frantz Fanon garnered attention in the United States, Sanford's novel depicted many of the psychosexual dynamics of racism and their disturbing links to the colonization process.[2] Fully five decades prior to the widespread discussion among scholars about "The Wages of Whiteness," an expression derived from W. E. B. Du Bois for the psychological and public benefits of race prejudice to white workers, Sanford depicted the doubled-edged and ultimately destructive consequences of these "wages" for their presumed beneficiaries.[3] An entire political generation before notions of the rights of armed self-defense and autonomous self-organization by people of color became broadly accepted by Euro-American radicals of the 1960s, Sanford's novel promoted a political response in which an African-American woman strikes the first blow for freedom in her own way, violently and with deference to no man.

From a literary perspective, this novel is revolutionary in form as well as content. In its art, *The People from Heaven* brilliantly fuses politics and technique, thus defying the classificatory systems promoted by a half century of literary critics. Yet the novel's authentic success as literature may have produced the terms for its commercial failure and, until now, its critical neglect; ironically, the "problem" with Sanford's novel is that it didn't fail in the ways that Marxist, modernist, or historical novels are *supposed* to fail in order to conform to these various genres as they were constructed.

That is, even though the author is a Marxist, *The People from Heaven* bears few of the alleged features of the "proletarian novel," or novels about strikes, "bottom dogs," middle-class decay, or conversions to socialism. Hence this work, and all others by Sanford, receive no mention in Walter Rideout's *Radical Novel in the United States* (1956), Daniel Aaron's *Writers on the Left* (1961), or any of the substantial scholarship devoted to that proletarian novel tradition usually associated with Mike Gold, Jack Conroy, and the early John Steinbeck. If Sanford's work had ended with the formation of a class-conscious trade union or the heroine picking up a copy of *The Communist Manifesto,* it would have at least received a passing reference in the substantial corpus of books and dissertations about the radical novel.

Moreover, even though the techniques of *The People from Heaven* are aggressively experimental—indeed, in many respects "modernist"—Sanford's antiracist and anticolonialist politics are far too central and "in your face" to allow the work to sit comfortably in the modernist genre conventionally represented by James Joyce, Franz Kafka, and William Faulkner, whose politics are often missed or misunderstood by readers. While some experimental novels with technical skill equivalent to Sanford's were produced by open leftists such as Henry Roth (*Call It Sleep,* 1934) and Nathanael West (*The Day of the Locust,* 1939), none are as direct, unambiguous, and unapologetic in their political message. Again, Sanford "failed" to attenuate his antiracism into what might be approached as an abstract or allegorical trope for the human condition.

Finally, as indicated by the novel's nine poetic commentaries on episodes of persecution and oppression from the fifteenth through nineteenth centuries, History is central to Sanford's understanding of the forces behind contemporary experience; in fact, *The People from Heaven* is partly a "critical realist" text in the way that the term was used by the Hungarian Marxist critic Georg Lukács.[4] Yet this is not a radical Historical Novel in the manner of outstanding Marxist-influenced works such as John Dos Passos's *U.S.A.* (1936), Howard Fast's *Freedom Road* (1944), or Margaret Walker's *Jubilee* (1966). *The People from Heaven* proceeds by meditation and a subtle pattern of association, not by relentless chronological development and systematic, thick descriptions of society. In Sanford's novel, the role of History is perhaps closest to that found in William Carlos Williams's essays in his collection *In the American Grain* (1925), albeit Sanford's excursions into the past are poetic and interspersed with a thematically related, taut fictional narrative covering events lasting about a week in the life of the town of Warrensburg. Once again, San-

ford "failed"—failed to employ the kind of convention-
al realism for which historical novelists such as Fast are
so often stigmatized as "middlebrow."[5]

Nevertheless, precisely due to the exhaustion of these
earlier theorizations of cultural tradition, the moment is
ripe in the 1990s for fresh discussions and appreciations
of *The People from Heaven*. At one time, these canonical
constructs of literary radicalism, modernism, and historical fiction may have been pathbreaking explications clar-
ifying specific currents within the larger literary stream,
but they now may also serve to obscure vital and note-
worthy works such as Sanford's. The past fifteen years
have witnessed a dramatic increase of students and scholars grappling to forge a broader and more complex cultural history. They have searched anew throughout many
facets of U.S. literary history for alternative "moments"
and paradigms, many of which engage precisely the issues central to Sanford's excoriating dramatization of
complex interconnections among racism, sexism, and
economic privilege and their roots in the history of the
United States.

✿

The author of *The People from Heaven* is as much an
"original" as the work itself. John Sanford, born Julian
Shapiro in New York City in 1904, is living testimony
to the continuity of the radical literary tradition from
the 1930s to the 1990s. At age ninety-one, Sanford, now
residing in Santa Barbara, recently completed his twen-
ty-first book, *The View from Mount Morris* (1994). His

twenty previous books, most of them honed to near per-
fection by a singular ability to unite stunning artistry and
undisguised social criticism, run the gamut from fiction
in the realist and naturalist mode, to historical poetry
and prose commentary, to novelized autobiography and
other experiments. *The People from Heaven* expresses a
distinct stage in the evolution of his craft, yet it stands
alone as a signal achievement within his oeuvre, as well
as in the various subgenres of U.S. literature to which it
has affinities.

The roots of his art stem from the remarkable cross-
currents of the late 1920s and early 1930s, when individuals such as Sanford responded to two trends in U.S. culture, fusing the modernist call to create a fresh language
with the radical call to take a stand on behalf of the ex-
ploited. The result was a brilliant flowering of literary
women and men, writers of color, and Euro-Americans.
These were people of the Left who consecrated their art
of fiction to social emancipation. Nelson Algren (*Somebody in Boots,* 1935), Arna Bontemps (*Black Thunder,*
1936), Edward Dahlberg (*Bottom Dogs,* 1930), James T.
Farrell (*Young Lonigan,* 1932), Langston Hughes (*The
Ways of White Folks,* 1934), Josephine Johnson (*Now in
November,* 1934), Meridel Le Sueur (*The Girl,* 1939),
Richard Wright (*Uncle Tom's Children,* 1938), and others
established an occasionally prominent but often hidden
cultural stream of literary radicalism of uneven quality
that would flow through subsequent decades until it was
overtaken by new styles of cultural rebellion with the
advent of the New Left of the 1960s. Although Sanford

was once part of this larger left-wing literary movement of the 1930s and 1940s, which more or less looked to the Communist party and the former Soviet Union for political inspiration, he is among the few who continued to write, and write well, while staying loyal to his fundamental political convictions in the fifty years that followed.

The son of a lawyer, and a lawyer himself by training, Sanford came under the spell of literature through his personal association with Nathanael West, to whom *The People from Heaven* is dedicated. It was West (born Weinstein) who suggested that his friend change his name, and so Julian Shapiro became John Sanford, the name of the protagonist in his first novel, *The Water-Wheel* (1933).

Unaffected initially by radical politics in his New York period, Sanford's move to Hollywood, following the minor commercial success of his brutally powerful novel *The Old Man's Place* (1935), put him in touch with the Communist movement. His connection with the movie industry also brought him immediately in contact with the screenwriter Marguerite Roberts (1905–89), to whom he was married for more than fifty years. Together they shared the ugly "Time of the Toad" of the Hollywood blacklist era that ended his film career and caused a major disruption of hers.

✿

Sanford's political history brings forward important new evidence concerning the controversial matter of U.S. writers and Communism. Due to the red-baiting that became the official line of the 1950s Thought Police running the educational institutions and the media (supervised by watchdogs of the FBI and demagogues of the House Committee on UnAmerican Activities), a social commitment that was once a badge of honor now became highly suspect. Any relationship to the Communist party, especially an organizational one, became something to be denied, repudiated, or, at least, minimized.

Later on, scholars hoping to redeem the artistic quality of certain writers once on the Left tended to dwell on whatever evidence might be found of their distance from the Communist party; to be briefly attracted to Communism, like Steinbeck or Dos Passos, might be regarded as compatible with the production of authentic literature, so long as the writer did not actually join or, at least, function loyally for any length of time. This approach reached the point of outright falsification of history when, in 1988, an effort to reclaim Richard Wright's *12 Million Black Voices* (1941) as a quality work of art in a new edition was accompanied by the statement that Wright "never actually joined" the Communist party.[6] Wright, in fact, was proudly public about his affiliation in the 1930s, and he wrote in detail about his Party experiences in later years.[7] Most recently, in a perhaps understandable but nevertheless oversimplified reaction to hostile and reductive treatments of Communism and writers, several scholarly books claim that the cultural movement associated with Communism produced no restrictions of significance in regard to a writer's technical approach or style.[8]

A study of Sanford's experience indicates that, in fact, the Communist movement definitely promoted a strong orientation toward certain literary styles and themes, and had various means of encouragement and discouragement. Imaginative works were frequently judged in reviews and public discussions according to political implications that might be attributed to an interpretation of certain passages and events in the narrative. The institutional mechanisms through which pressure was exerted came through variations of the famous Hollywood "Writers Clinic," led by the Communist playwright and film writer John Howard Lawson, where draft manuscripts were read and reviewed by a committee of Party members. There were also critical notices in the Communist press by leading Party spokespersons, who were sometimes full-time, paid staff members and who held posts on cultural commissions. Less formally, it was not unusual for individuals close to or in the Party to voluntarily share their manuscripts with comrades, especially those who had already published and who were seen as more politically developed, and to welcome feedback of a political or literary nature.

But Sanford's experience demonstrates that it was not always required that one accede to changes proposed through such institutional constraints, so long as one was otherwise politically and organizationally loyal. In the case of *The People from Heaven,* a draft of the work was judged ultra-Left, and even too Black Nationalist, by members of a Los Angeles committee.[9] This was not surprising in the context of the wartime patriotic orientation that the Communist movement was then promoting. Nevertheless, Sanford refused to alter a word of the manuscript, which was also his policy in dealing with criticism from publishing houses.

In my view, it would be a mistake either to ignore Sanford's specifically Communist political commitments or to try to reduce his novel to a mere function of them, a dramatization of ideology. The overwhelming evidence available from biographical studies of writers, as well as specific evidence from Sanford's own memoirs, indicates that a work of imaginative literature grows primarily out of the unconscious or, in Sanford's words, from an "unknown retrieval system."[10]

On the other hand, Sanford's choice of theme, his political categories, and the antiracist values that shine through on every page cannot be disassociated from his Marxist views. His was not a textbook Marxism but a Marxism of a general character. In his literary work, it was an identification with the underdog against the oppressor, not a Marxism dictated by the U.S. Communist party. His own memory that he "wasn't writing for the Party but out of my own beliefs and sympathy" is confirmed by both the individualistic qualities of the literature itself and the absence of any evidence that Party cultural leaders ever desired to promote him as a figure to emulate in the way that Howard Fast and several others were lionized.[11]

This is not to suggest, however, that Sanford was not really a "left-wing writer" or a legitimate part of the Communist cultural tradition in the United States. In a

1947 argument with a Party cultural leader who insisted that *The People from Heaven* was "antisocial" because "it ends with a black woman blowing a white man's brains out," Sanford retorted that he was in his own way true to the much-contested Communist slogan, "Art is a weapon." He insisted, "If that book isn't a weapon, I never saw one."[12]

However, some parts of *The People from Heaven* originated in stories written from Sanford's pre-Marxist phase; in particular, the narrative of the adulterous minister, "Bishop's Story," which was previously published as "Once in a Sedan and Twice Standing Up."[13] In addition, the novel was partly connected to an earlier novel set in the same region, *Seventy Times Seven* (1939), through several characters that he retained. While sketching in the opening vignettes of these and a range of others to populate his fictionalized Warrensburg, Sanford found himself writing the word "Brothers" as the beginning of a sermon by the preacher, Dan Hunter. This was followed by the image of a Black woman walking into a white man's store on a cold, rainy night to be greeted by, "You want anything, nigger?"[14]

Some of the other autobiographical elements behind the construction of the text have more explicitly radical associations. Sanford had been haunted for some time by an empathy with the Native Americans who thought the Europeans were "the people from Heaven," and he wanted "to write of the hell they brought along."[15] He was also troubled by memories of his attempt to hitchhike through the Carolinas when he ran away from home at age sixteen; when asked by a man how he felt about the South, Sanford found himself complaining about the lynchings of Blacks, and then the name of Leo Frank, a Jew who was also lynched, came into his mind, suggesting some degree of subconscious identity as a Jew who might be conceivably persecuted as were Blacks. Beyond this, the drive to write *The People from Heaven* seems connected with guilt Sanford felt over his failure to be aware of the execution of Sacco and Vanzetti, when Sanford was twenty-four.[16]

In any event, the reception of the novel in the public press did not evidence the simplistic equations between the art and Sanford's politics in the way that scholars of later generations would indict and dismiss the literary movement allied with the Communist party. By and large the response was characterized by a failure to know what to do with the novel. Most reviewers saw many strong qualities in the language and style, although there were complaints that these were not consistently sustained. While most critics also noted the political implications, they did not dismiss the author as a propagandist. What is striking is the inability of the reviewers to come up with many novels for comparison, contemporary or historical. Moreover, when the critics failed to find a context, they seemed unable to recognize that something truly pathbreaking had been produced.[17]

As a result, the richness and complexity of Sanford's vision—the pattern of symbols, the lush allusiveness, the mythological aura—were inadequately recognized and acknowledged. Unfortunately, these very features can preclude a mass audience from spontaneously embracing a work without aggressive intervention by literary critics. Earlier, the left-wing, antiracist satire of Erskine Caldwell in a book such as *Tobacco Road* (1932) was sufficiently direct and straightforward to reach a large public on its own, especially in the political atmosphere of the early Depression. In contrast, *The People from Heaven,* published and reviewed well into World War II, was not by itself able to locate and inspire a popular audience.

However, Sanford's innovative and powerfully focused artistic techniques should have earned from critics and scholars the respect accorded to a Faulkner or some other writer whose "difficulty" (a vague category that varies from reader to reader, depending on prior knowledge and experience as well as one's frame of mind when reading the text) was a mark of high craft. This wonderfully jarring juxtaposition—of the powerful "simplicity" of Sanford's angry antiracism with the necessity of reading *The People from Heaven* carefully, with attention to detail and an active involvement in constructing meaning—produced an unfamiliar blend that seems to have rendered its critics of 1943–44 incapable of providing a clear perspective on its meaning and significance.

✿

From the opening scene, as Dan Hunter surveys a congregation comprised of dated tombstones (the dates incomplete for those still living), to the complex finale among the ruins of Dan's burned-out church, the readers of *The People from Heaven* are pulled in many directions. We are taken on a tour of sensory and intellectual experiences unlike those produced by any other text in U.S. literature. In the most accessible parts of the narrative, we are presented, following the introduction of much of the Warrensburg community through vignettes, with the appearance of a mysterious stranger.

An unknown and unnamed African-American woman arrives in a tight-knit, repressed, authoritarian community where the chief shopkeeper, Eli Bishop, is arch lecher and thug. Her appearance divides the town, forcing all to take sides. The miniature civil war that follows is connected with a number of subplots that bring to the fore anti-Indian prejudice, sexism, hypocrisy, and anti-Semitism. Undergirding the whole novel is a powerful examination of the historical roots of the ugly racism lying beneath the superficial harmony of a rural community and the mechanisms by which it is fed by sexual repression and passed on from parents (usually the fathers) to children (usually the sons).

At the same time, Sanford employs nine historical inserts to propel us back into a sequence of events between 1492 and 1863: the journey of Columbus to the New World (1492); the experiences of Pocahontas with the Europeans (1607); the arrival of a Dutch man o' war with twenty captive Africans (1619); a recreation of native peoples welcoming whites as "the people from Heaven" (dated 1620); a scene from the religious conflict between Christians and native peoples (1632); the witchcraft trials (1691); an imaginary dialogue called "God in the Hands of an Angry Sinner" (1741); a slave escape (1775); and the story of a former slave who decides to serve the Union army as a spy in the South (1863).

To some readers, who are accustomed to apprehending history as the presentation of "fact," these may well be troubling aspects of the novel. After all, Sanford's poetic commentaries refer to known episodes, yet they are refracted through the individual sensibility of the author. What, the reader may ask, is "mere" opinionated interpretation and what is "real"? Indeed, a number of editors who rejected the book for publication and critics who commented on the version that was released by Harcourt, Brace and Company wished the historical commentaries had been removed.

Today, however, Sanford's strategy here appears more like that of a sophisticated, modern Marxist who has learned something from critics of the Enlightenment and even from the poststructuralists: that the boundaries between "objective fact" and "imposed narration" are not always clear but are contested by the values of the storyteller, whether in prose or poetry, history or imaginative literature. Like the Marxist playwright Bertolt Brecht, whose aim was to agitate the minds of his audience rather than encourage passive identification and purgation, Sanford encourages readers to think for themselves, to doubt and be vigilant.

A third complicating feature is that the narrative, while propelled along at times with the power of a detective thriller, also crosses over into modernism; it is self-consciously experimental in form and can be difficult and disturbing. At times there are unannounced transitions, in setting and character, from "reality" to "fantasy." Moreover, episodes in the "story" line seem to have suggestive links to many of the historical inserts that precede them, but it is left to the reader to conjecture the precise relationship or simply intuit a more elusive connection.

For example, the insert about the "discovery" of the Americas is followed by the white men of Warrensburg "discovering" and trying to "name" the Black woman; the insert about the persecution of witches is followed by an episode where America Smith is persecuted for her race; the insert depicting a slave escape is followed by a scene where the American Indian father, Bigelow Vroom, seizes a rifle to defend his son, Aben, against Bishop and another racist; and the insert about the former slave going to spy on the Confederacy is followed by America Smith's decision to enter Eli Bishop's house to confront him. Virtually the entire text is carefully and complexly interwoven and interrelated in a series of associations, prefigurings, and other devices.[18] Nevertheless, for the casual reader there are mysteries, and it is fair to predict that students and scholars of the text will have many opportunities to engage in discussion and debate.

A fourth feature of special concern to today's readers may be the Jewish-specific aspects of this novel about anti-Black racism, depicting a rebel African-American female protagonist. At the excruciatingly high-pitched, violent climax of *The People from Heaven,* Sanford describes an unforgettably symptomatic showdown. The altercation is between the racist demagogue Eli Bishop and the tiny number of Warrensburg dissidents. First Bishop bashes Dan Hunter, the iconoclastic town preacher; then he pounds unconscious Bigelow Vroom, the proud American Indian. Standing over his victims, Bishop turns on the terrorized onlookers:

> "An hour after he can walk," he said, nodding back at Vroom, "we're going to have a parade in this town, and he's going to head it."
>
> He stooped to pick up a pine cone. "It'll start at the Post Office, and it'll keep moving till it's out of sight. There'll be four people marching in that parade: this Indian here, the Indian's boy-bastard Aben, the nigger-woman, and one more." He cracked a few scales from the cone and let them fall. "The Jew." He looked now at Novinsky. "The Jew son-of-a-bitch: he goes too. This use to be a white man's town, Warrensburg, and it won't be long before it's white all over again." A butterfly beat past, its speckled wings applauding.
>
> America Smith was a grave-length away, her hands, as if in a muff, hidden by the drape of the spare dress. She brought one of them forth, and the black accusation of the Colt was leveled at Bishop. "Run," she said.
>
> "Put that gun down, nigger!"
>
> "Now pray and run."
>
> "Did you hear me, nig . . . !"
>
> A bullet stopped Bishop's last syllable at his teeth, and teeth tumbled from a second mouth that opened in the back of his head. A dead man did a half-twist, gave at the joints, and collapsed.

Still holding the Colt, the woman polled the faces of the crowd. . . .[19]

I call this episode symptomatic because it typifies many characteristic features of the Jewish-American literary use of an African-American rebel protagonist in the tradition forged by the mid-century, Communist-led cultural Left. The author is Jewish and writes from a Jewish subject position, but the viewpoint is not, at least not consciously, Judeocentric, Jewish nationalist, or Jewish particularist.[20] The main agent of revenge or retribution, America Smith, is African American, although the presence of Native American targets of racism and agents of resistance, Bigelow and Aben Vroom, is by no means a casual addition.

The Jewish character, Abe Novinsky, while not among the primary cast of actors in earlier sections, has been referred to in passing. Barely tolerated by the community, Novinsky lives on the borders of racial ostracism. Thus the sudden shift in focus to him by Bishop, which is at first a bit surprising, is not, on second thought, illogical. Indeed, the anti-Semitism of the community has been adequately foreshadowed so that this inclusion of the Jew with the persecuted characters of color germinates new meanings for which seeds were planted in earlier episodes.

Moreover, the introduction of Novinsky as a potential victim just before America Smith downs Bishop strongly presses toward the following political allegory:

1. Native fascism has its origins in the successful con-

quest and victimization of indigenous peoples (represented by Vroom), which religious and other Euro-American community leaders (represented by Hunter) failed
to halt.

2. The latest group of targets, African Americans
(represented by America Smith), must learn the lessons
of the past and not rely on others, and they must be prepared to defend themselves with arms, if necessary.

3. It is in the interest of all others who are oppressed,
first among them Jews (represented by Novinsky), to
defend without qualifications the African American
struggle in the United States because, if the racists are
successful against the Blacks, they will next turn on others, starting with Jews.

Sanford's climax makes this perspective more explicit
than many similar texts.[21] But even here the complex
relationship must be understood as part of a larger Marxist-
internationalist outlook. The Jewish-Black relation is not
the fulcrum, or single explanatory factor, of this fairly
substantial tradition of Jewish radical writers culturally
"cross-dressing" so as to present their themes through
African-American rebel-protagonists. It would be a vi-
olation of the known intent, and the information we
have about the art of John Sanford, to center his Jew-
ishness as "the" explanatory factor for the artistic and
ideological text. It would also violate the character of the
whole subtradition of Jewish radical novelists combat-
ing racial capitalism through Black protagonists.

Of course, some Jewish elements are present in the
text, as they are in Sanford's self-consciousness as a writ-

er. But *The People from Heaven* is overdetermined by his 1930s radicalization, not to mention myriad idiosyncratic matters of personal psychology and literary influence. For such biographical/artistic as well as political reasons, it is probably "no accident," as we Marxists are always pontificating, that *The People from Heaven* contains the Jewish character Abe Novinsky, whose tale of a pogrom is a sensational episode.[22] It is also probably "no accident" that, as the arch bigot Eli Bishop ascends to power at the novel's climax, it is his anti-Semitism that triggers his demise at the hands of America Smith.[23]

This said about the combined possible artistic, biographical, and political motivations, it is important to note that such a climax to the novel was a personal choice of Sanford's—one that was denounced as ultra-Left and ultra-Black Nationalist by the Communist party committee that read the draft manuscript of his book. As in the case of Guy Endore, whose novel *Babouk* was likewise sharply criticized as Black Nationalist, in Endore's case by an African-American Communist critic in the *New Masses*,[24] Sanford was expressing an anger and empathy that preceded and transcended any formal adherence to "party line."[25]

☼

That John Sanford's uncompromising dissection of racism should be republished after fifty years of obscurity is hardly an innocent or accidental "return of the repressed." The values and behavior dramatized by Sanford are endemic to and long-term features of our country and its culture. Moreover, contemporary trends in literary studies have paved the way for the novel's reception and appreciation by a new generation of students, scholars, and general readers.

Its reappearance confirms the analysis of Marxist critics such as Raymond Williams about the social mechanisms by which some books are remembered and others forgotten.[26] Ideologically and artistically, Sanford's novel raises many of the cutting-edge questions about the selective construction of canons and traditions in a liberal democracy. Our refusal to let this book die reinforces the assessment of scholars such as Cary Nelson who insist that what has been correspondingly silenced in this institutionalized process are often works exploring issues beyond the perimeters of acceptable political discourse.[27] As feminist critics have demonstrated in the case of "lost" writings such as Tillie Olsen's *Yonondio* (begun in 1934; published in 1974), Meridel Le Sueur's *The Girl* (1939), and Josephine Herbst's *Rope of Gold* (1939), such issues can anticipate later concerns, often approached from perspectives far in advance of contemporaries.[28]

## NOTES

1. Several of Sanford's novels and short stories use an Adirondack setting; six of them are collected in *Adirondack Stories* (Santa Barbara: Capra Press, 1976).

2. See Frantz Fanon, *Black Skin, White Masks* (New York: Grove, 1967), and *The Wretched of the Earth* (New York: Grove, 1965).

3. While earlier writers touched on the issue, David Roe-

diger brought the "white problem" to national attention in his compelling study *The Wages of Whiteness: Race and the Making of the American Working Class* (London: Verso, 1991).

4. According to Lukács, a twentieth-century "realist" work does not simply "mirror" history but offers a perspective compatible with socialist principles of interpretation on the crises of modern society. See Georg Lukács, *The Meaning of Contemporary Realism* (London: Merlin, 1963).

5. Leslie Fiedler writes: "Fast is particularly interesting as the last full-time bard of the [Communist] movement, its most faithful middlebrow servant in the arts" (*To the Gentiles* [New York: Stein and Day, 1971], p. 100).

6. David Bradley, "Preface," in Richard Wright, *12 Million Black Voices* (1941; rpt., New York: Thunder's Mouth Press, 1988), p. xiv.

7. The most complete version of Wright's description of his experiences is now contained in *American Hunger* (New York: Harper, 1977); more accurate details can be found in Michel Fabre, *The Unfinished Quest of Richard Wright* (Urbana: University of Illinois Press, 1993).

8. See James F. Murphy, *The Proletarian Moment: The Controversy over Leftism in Literature* (Urbana: University of Illinois Press, 1991), and Barbara Foley, *Radical Representations* (Durham: Duke University Press, 1993). For a detailed critique of the former, see Alan Wald, "Literary Leftism Reconsidered," *Science and Society* 57, no. 2 (Summer 1993): 214–22.

9. In *A Very Good Land to Fall With*, vol. 3 of *Scenes from the Life of an American Jew* (Santa Rosa: Black Sparrow Press, 1987), Sanford recalls a fall 1941 meeting with a Party literary committee to which he had been "directed" to submit *The People from Heaven*. He claims that he was told to make revisions to eliminate what the committee believed was the book's call to a premature armed revolt against whites (pp. 202–3).

10. Interview with John Sanford, July 30, 1989, Santa Barbara, Calif.

11. Ibid.

12. John Sanford, *A Walk in the Fire* (Santa Rosa: Black Sparrow Press, 1989), p. 79.

13. The story appeared in the third and last issue of *Contact*, in December 1932.

14. Sanford, *A Very Good Land to Fall With*, pp. 176–83 passim.

15. Ibid., p. 163.

16. See references in Sanford, *A Very Good Land to Fall With*, pp. 162, 174, 175, and John Sanford, *The Color of the Air* (Santa Rosa: Black Sparrow Press, 1985), p. 109.

17. Naturally, there were passing references to the possible influence of William Carlos Williams's *In the American Grain* (1925; rpt., New York: New Directions, 1956) for the historical commentaries and Edgar Lee Masters's *Spoon River Anthology* (1915) for the brief but candid biographical sketches. See Iris Barry, "On Small-Town Morality," *New York Herald Tribune Weekly Book Review*, 2 Jan. 1944, 44; "Briefly Noted," *New Yorker*, Oct. 30, 1943, 81; Philip Van Doren Stern, "Sanford's Varorium," *Saturday Review of Literature* 26 (Nov. 13, 1943): 13; John Hyde Preston, "From the Still Center," *New Republic* 109 (Dec. 13, 1943): 859; Mark Schorer, "Assorted White Trash," *New York Times*, Oct. 31, 1943, 12.

18. Tery Griffin has done an impressive job of correlating the commentaries to dramatic episodes. See "Fiction Wound in Reality: History in the Work of John Sanford" (paper prepared for graduate seminar, University of Michigan, Fall 1993).

19. John Sanford, *The People from Heaven* (1943; rpt., Urbana: University of Illinois Press, 1995), pp. 230–31.

20. Harold Cruse has argued that virtually all attempts by Jewish-American Communists to write about African Americans are, in fact, expressions of Jewish chauvinism. See *The Crisis of the Negro Intellectual* (New York: William Morrow, 1967).

21. A few of the many novels by Jewish-American radicals

featuring Black protagonists are Maxwell Bodenheim, *Ninth Avenue* (1925); Laura Caspary, *The White Girl* (1929); Guy Endore, *Babouk* (1934); Len Zinberg, *Walk Hard, Talk Loud* (1940); Benjamin Appel, *The Dark Stain* (1943); Howard Fast, *Freedom Road* (1944); David Alman, *The Hourglass* (1947); and Earl Conrad, *Rock Bottom* (1954) and *Gulf Stream North* (1954).

22. When Novinsky describes how naked Jewish girls were shot from trees, he strongly underscores the novel's theme of the interrelationship of sexual domination and racial hatred—something about which the reader might think even more after Eli Bishop rapes the Black woman as the culmination of his persecution of her.

23. At the least, one might conjecture that Sanford was dramatizing, at the moment of Nazi expansionism, how the uprooting of anti-Black racism in the United States now, "by any means necessary," might prevent its logical escalation into other forms of persecution. America Smith's courageous action should also be supported because it is justified by the failure of others to take steps earlier.

24. See the discussion of this episode in Alan Wald, "The Subaltern Speaks," *Monthly Review*, April 1992, 17–29.

25. That the intensity of personal feelings about racism came before and superseded ideology is documented by an incident in the late fall of 1941, shortly after the Communist party threw itself into the war effort. At that time an official of the Party committee that read the manuscript calmly explained to Sanford: "[The book is] a plain incitement to revolt, and in the conditions of the day, a revolt would fail." Sanford bluntly replied: "Appomattox was seventy-five years back . . . . If I were black, I wouldn't want to wait another seventy-five for the right to piss in the toilet of my choice" (Sanford, *A Very Good Land to Fall With*, p. 203).

26. The most compelling explanation of traditions and canons remains Raymond Williams's *Marxism and Literature* (Oxford: Oxford University Press, 1977).

27. See Cary Nelson, *Repression and Recovery* (Madison: University of Wisconsin Press, 1989).

28. See Constance Coiner, "Literature of Resistance: The Intersection of Feminism and the Communist Left in Meridel Le Sueur and Tillie Olsen," in *Left Politics and the Literary Profession,* ed. Lennard Davis and M. Bella Mirabella (New York: Columbia University Press, 1990), pp. 162–85; Elinor Langer, *Josephine Herbst: The Story She Could Never Tell* (Boston: Atlantic, 1984); Paula Rabinowitz, *Labor and Desire: Women's Revolutionary Fiction in Depression America* (Chapel Hill: University of North Carolina Press, 1991); Deborah Rosenfelt, "From the Thirties: Tillie Olsen and the Radical Tradition," *Feminist Studies* 7 (Fall 1981): 370–406.

# BIBLIOGRAPHY

## REVIEWS OF *THE PEOPLE FROM HEAVEN*

Barry, Iris. "On Small-Town Morality." *New York Herald Tribune Weekly Book Review,* Jan. 2, 1944, 8.
"Briefly Noted." *New Yorker,* Oct. 30, 1943, 81.
Preston, John Hyde. "From the Still Center." *New Republic* 109 (Dec. 13, 1943): 859.
*Saturday Review of Literature,* Dec. 19, 1925, 425.
Schorer, Mark. "Assorted White Trash." *New York Times,* Oct. 31, 1943, 12.
Stern, Philip Van Doren. "Sanford's Varorium." *Saturday Review of Literature* 26 (Nov. 13, 1943): 13.

## SOURCES ON JOHN SANFORD

### PUBLISHED

Sanford, John. *A Very Good Land to Fall With.* Vol. 3 of *Scenes from the Life of an American Jew.* Santa Rosa: Black Sparrow Press, 1989.

Smith, Robert W. "An Interview with John Sanford: An American Classic." *Literary Review* 28 (Summer 1985): 544–54.

Williams, William Carlos, and John Sanford. *A Correspondence.* Santa Barbara: Oyster Press, 1984.

### UNPUBLISHED

Griffin, Tery. "Fiction Wound in Reality: History in the Work of John Sanford." Essay prepared for a graduate seminar on radical culture in the United States, fall 1993, University of Michigan, Ann Arbor.

Wald, Alan. Interview with John Sanford. Santa Barbara, Calif., July 30, 1989.

### ADDITONAL SOURCES

Martin, Jay. *Nathanael West: The Art of His Life.* New York: Farrar, Straus and Giroux, 1970.

Williams, William Carlos. *In the American Grain.* 1925. New York: New Directions, 1956.

The People from Heaven

# THE SEVENTH DAY

DANIEL HUNTER stood in the entry of the church, listening to the final bronze shimmers ripple from the bell-loft and crawl away on the moist morning air. All but one of his congregation were in their pews, and the one—Doc Slocum—had just limped into sight on the path leading up from the Warrensburg pike to the churchyard on Number Four Pond. Hunter watched the old man make his stiff crustacean way along the bank, twice coughing and twice spitting upon the quiet water, but as he neared the foot of the steps, the preacher went down to help him mount them, one by one, like a child.

The sun still overshot the pond-hollow, which lay in the shade like a warm dish cooling, but soon the rising steam would dwindle to lint and then to nothing, and the water, sun-struck, would be a clean perforation in the body of the earth. Turning to the pulpit, Hunter's eyes took with them a last panoramic swivel of images: a long shed filled with wagons and muddied motor-

3

cars; the night-washed lawn of the parsonage; a wedge of cemetery between the two buildings; and the damp spikes of the cemetery fence, each burning like a black candle kindled by the sun.

Hunter split his Bible at a place-ribbon, and putting his hands on the cold pages, he looked out through the open double-doors at a blue-blast of water behind the faces of the congregation—at the pond, another and now glaring face that filled the little meeting-house with running glances of light and shadow. Standing very still, Hunter was mobile in this shifting dapple, like a stone in a stream.

"Brothers . . . ," he said, and then he waited for feet to be settled and voices silent.

Several rows ahead of Doc Slocum, who had taken a seat on the last bench in the left section, the celluloid collar worn by Emerson Polhemus supported a cornice of withered neck. Between Polhemus and the huddle of skulls in the front pews—the back hair and the hats, the wigs and the shining scalps—three others sat unattached: Eli Bishop, Aaron Platt, and Grace Tennent Paulhan. All faces were aimed at the pulpit, but as if the intervening bone and the pink flesh and the balanced bowls of paper fruit did not exist, Slocum saw them from behind, scooped out and in reverse, each the concave of a dangling mask. Among these living, he saw the faces of six dead and gone to powder in the ground, and once, only once—when he thought of a dog named Banjo, dead too—a smile became a brief dazzle on the mask of his own face. . . .

4

## EMERSON POLHEMUS

### b. 1875-

"Emerson," I said, "I want to ask you something. Can you name anybody that'd mourn you if you died?"

He said, "No."

I said, "Doesn't that worry you?"

He said, "No."

I said, "It'd worry *me*."

"Would it?" he said. "Why?"

"I'd hate to feel I overstayed my welcome."

"I ain't so shy, Doc. I could live a extra fifty years on spite alone."

## ELI BISHOP

### b. 1907-

I said, "Eli, how is it you never get sick?"

"I'm like a bear-steak," he said. "The more you chew me, the bigger I get."

"I haven't made a quarter off you since the day you were born."

"You won't make nothing the day I die. I'll go out fighting and faunching."

"And fornicating."

"If I'm lucky—fornicating."

"Luck, hell! You're as randy a cock as ever rode a pullet."

He ran four fingers of each hand up the underside of my lapels. "Always figured they'd have to bury me face-down, Doc," he said.

I shrugged him off. "What're you doing in town today?"

"Well, to tell the truth, I was feeling kind of loppy this morning," he said. "K-i-n-d of loppy, Doc."

"Thank God!" I said. "Come on in the office!"

"What for?" he said, tightening my bow-tie. "You got a woman in there?"

## EDNA PIRIE

### b. 1880-

I said, "You ought to take a day off. You're dead on your feet."

"Good," she said. "I'll walk to my own funeral."

"That'll be about six months from now, Edna. I'm warning you."

"The sooner, the better," she said. "I can't wait to see Warrensburg's face when it reads my stone: 'Forget the Resurrection, Almighty God; I need the sleep.'"

## ESTHER PIRIE PELL

### b. 1898-d. 1922

*She weighed 126 when she married Trubee Pell, and the day they sent him to Dannemora, she weighed 83 soaking wet when she was fished out of the Schroon, but I'm a three-cornered liar if she wasn't prettier dead than a live woman sleeping.*

## SAM (tb.) PIRIE

### b. 1877-

I said, "How's Edna?"
He said, "Still eating."
I said, "And still working?"
He said, "Well, she's still eating."
"Get dressed and get out, Sam."
"First I want to know how I'm feeling."
"A damn sight better than your wife—and she's got *two* lungs."
"It's worth a dollar to hear that," he said, offering me a cart-wheel.
"Shove it!" I said.
He chucked the money on my desk. "*You* shove it," he said. "I don't owe nobody a cent."

## WALTER PELL

### *b. 1868-d. 1938*

*I said, "You'll have to take it easier, Walt. A watch has only so many ticks in it, and no more."*

*He said, "I ain't lived all this time for nothing, Doc. They'll let him out some day, and he'll come back. He'll come back, Doc."*

## TRUBEE PELL

### b. 1895-

"Trubee!"
"Doc!"

"My God, Trubee! My God, how long has it been?"

"I think you folks celebrated the birth of Jesus Christ seventeen times while I was up in that cell on Lake Champlain."

"Seventeen times!" I said. "Aren't we the religious bastards, though?"

"Yes," he said.

"Let me look you over, son."

"Only if you promise to tell me the truth. . . ."

. . . I told him after a while. "I love you," I said, "but I don't have the right medicine. They killed you up in that hole, Trubee! Trubee, they damn well killed you!"

All he said was, "Where's Pop laying?"

### LELAND POLK

#### b. 1894-

I said, "I thought I told you to wear that truss."

He said, "I give it to my dog."

"If you keep on with that heavy lifting, your guts are going to fall out in your lap."

"Hell, Doc," he said, "I got this hernia from raising prices, and don't ever think I didn't."

### JEROME PIPER

#### b. 1900-

He said, "When a man can't come away from the Widder's without crutches, it's high time she was run out of town."

8

"Listen," I said, "you got your limp stomping the high-road down to Saratoga!"

"I got it right here off of Gracie Paulhan!"

"Grace Paulhan's fresher than a blade of grass! I know, because I keep her that way. Why in hell do you think I go up there every night after business-hours? To give her some business of my own? I go to clean up the mess that Warrensburg makes!"

"Easy, Doc! That ain't made of rubber!"

"Lie still, you witch-burner!"


### DOLLY PIPER

b. 1902-

I said, "How do you feel, Dolly?"

"Fine, Doc," she said. "Why?"

"You want to stay that way?"

"Sure I do."

"Then go up to Riparius and board with your sister for a couple of weeks."

"Has he got it again, Doc?"

"Make it a month, just to be on the safe side."


### HERBERT ESTES

b. 1885-

I said, "How's the grave-digging business, Herb?"

"Slow," he said. "People ain't dying like they use to."

9

"Why don't you make it worth their while?"

"Doc, I'm offering the best thirty-dollar burial in Warren County, and I ain't sold one in a month."

"Some customers want a lot for their money."

"I give it to them. Why, I'm even featuring a coffin called the 'Barrymore'!"

"Cheer up. You'll have some new trade any day now."

"Glad to hear it, Doc. Do I know the party?"

"Not as well as you should, Herb."

PEARL HUSTIS

b. 1905-

She brought her daughter down to the office, saying, "What's the matter with Anna Mae, Doc? All the time she goes around sick at her stomach and throwing up— and my Arthur ain't got the build to stand for much more of it."

I said, "How long's Anna Mae been carrying on like this, Pearl?"

"Oh, four-five months, maybe."

It didn't take a wizard to come up with an opinion: all I had to do was put my hand on the girl's belly.

"A baby!" Pearl said. "Why, my God, Steve, the child ain't but fourteen!"

"You should've told that to the hired-man."

"*What* hired-man? Arthur works the place himself. . . ."

## ARTHUR HUSTIS

### b. 1899-

Anna Mae came down again the next day, but this time her father was with her.

"Doc," he said, "I want you to fix it so's the kid don't drop that foal."

"Wait out in the hall, will you, Anna Mae?" I said, and after the door had closed, I sat down at my desk and moved the controller of the electric-fan to 'LOW': the breeze made fingers in my hair. "What am I supposed to say to you, Art?"

"Nothing," he said. "Just boil your cutlery."

"If this were a world I could run like a set of toy-trains," I said, "I'd pour you a glass of rye and poison and watch you die."

"It ain't that kind of a world, though."

"What kind is it, Art?" I said. "What kind is it?"

He twisted his neck, pulling at his collar as if it were buttoned. "It's a place where decent people do the God-damnedest things," he said. "It's a place where you start out by kissing and wind up by sucking blood. Jesus! Jesus!"

I went to the door. "You can come in now, honey," I said.

### ANNA MAE HUSTIS

### b. 1925-d. 1939

*Septicemia.*

## HANNAH HARNED

### b. 1898-

"Just dropped in to pass the time of day," she said.

"That's mighty nice of you, Hannah," I said. "How's your old man?"

"I'm glad you brung that up, Doc. Tell the truth, that husband of mine's got me frazzled. He don't eat enough to keep a snow-bird alive."

"How do you like my new wall-paper?"

"He's getting so pore he has to find something to lean against to make a shadow."

"Did the kids have a good winter?"

"Honest to God, Doc, he has to stand up twice before you know he ain't setting."

"What did you think of Dan's sermon last Sunday?"

"And nervish! Why, he can be sleeping good for a while, and then all at once he pulls together like a mouse-trap and like to throw himself out of bed. What do you think I ought to do for him, Doc?"

"God damn it, Hannah!" I said. "You ought to steal a dollar from yourself and give it to him for a medical examination!"

## ASH HARNED

### b. 1896-

I said, "Where's the dollar, Ash?"

He brought the bill out of his pocket as if it were a strip of adhesive-tape plastered on his thigh.

I said, "Thanks, Ash."

12

"Doc," he said, "I'm a awful sick man."

"What makes you think so?"

"Ain't got no more flesh onto me than a pair of pliers."

"Why don't you eat?"

"Food costs money," he said. "When I think about it, honest to God you couldn't drive a prune into me with a mallet."

"Maybe," I said, "but I'll give you back your dollar if you let me try."

## BUELL HARNED

*b. 1920-d. 1922*

*Rickets.*

## SELMA FRENCH

b. 1892-

"Night after night," she said, "it's like he's trying to bury himself, like he's a dog digging a hole for a bone, but I'm forty-nine years old, Doc, forty-nine years old, and there's things the matter inside of me, and I can't bring myself to tell him because he's got his heart set on being a father, and he might run me out in the road if he knew I couldn't have a baby, and I love him, Doc, and I don't want him to be mad at me, so please help me, Doc, please do something, please give me a medicine to put in his coffee so he won't be plowing over tired old ground every night, every night, every night! Please have pity, Doc! I ain't got the

13

green touch—I never even could make flowers grow. *Please*, Doc!"

## ABEL FRENCH

### b. 1905-

"It's eating the life out of me, Doc," he said. "Me and Selma been married twelve years now, and we still ain't got a kid."

"That's too bad, Abe," I said. "As a father, you sound as if you'd take the toys off the Christmas-tree."

"Father?" he said. "All I want is to stop the boys laughing behind my back!"

## EDOM SMEAD

### b. 1885-

I said, "They tell me you've got the Indian locked up again."

He haha-ed on his star and polished it with his sleeve, saying, "I don't like Indians, Doc."

"I told you to let old Big Nose alone."

"You ain't sheriff, Doc."

"Turn him out, Ed. He's a friend of mine."

"He's tighter than a seal," he said. "Go home and roll yourself some pills."

"Turn him out," I said, "or, by God, this town's going to know that I'm not giving you shots for diabetes!"

"Okay, Doc," he said. "Okay."

14

## BIG NOSE

*b. ?-d. 1931*

*Booze.*

## HELEN SMEAD

b. 1895-

"You aren't sick, Helen," I said. "You just don't give a damn whether you live or die."

"Why should I?" she said.

"Because you're on the good side of forty, and handsome as a full-grown birch."

"I wish I wasn't. Then Ed'd give me a divorce without making me spill his misery all over Warrensburg."

"You don't need a divorce to move over to Tom Quinn's," I said. "Just a wagon."

"I wanted to hear you say that, Doc," she said. "How much do I owe you?"

"Nothing, Helen. It was a pleasure."

## TOMBIGBEE QUINN

b. 1890-

"Well, Professor," I said, "what would you do if the Board took your school away?"

"Keep on living."

"In sin?"

"*We* don't think it's sin, Doc."

## SLOCUM QUINN
### b. 1931-

"I think I have a pretty name," she said.

## JOHN LITTLEJOHN
### b. 1841-

"Daddy," I said, "you're the cutest old man in the State of New York."

"Wipe your nose and run along, bub," he said, "or I'll tell you what I had for breakfast one day at a place called Antietam."

"I'm crazy about you, Daddy, so you can tell me all over again."

"You really like me, boy?"

"Yes, Daddy, I do."

"Then make me live to be a hundred years old!" he said. "I ain't afraid to die—I get nearer to that every day I live—but when I was a kid I asked my Ma how old people grow to be, and she said a hundred, and every year I use to figure out how far I had to run, and I sort of kept on doing that all my life, and I was a old old man before I realized that numbers that started out as big as fish was getting to be small as fry—seven more to go, six, five, four, three. . . . I'm so near a hundred now, Doc! I'm so near it'd be a shame if that little fool dream didn't come true. Keep me going, Doc—promise you'll keep me going!"

"Daddy," I said, "you'll see a hundred if I have to go up in person and talk God into it!"

## JOEL CONFREY

### b. 1894-

"You've broken your hand, Joel," I said. "Who's the other feller?"

"My wife," he said.

"I've got a good mind to swat you with this splint."

"She was always hanging crosses around the child's neck," he said, "little brass crosses that she got off of that sneaking Vermont priest, Father Agnew. The child didn't know what they was or what they stood for— she just worn them, that's all. She'd play with them in her fingers, and sometimes she'd put them in her mouth and suck on them, and then when I tried to talk to her, damn if she wasn't slobbering over that hunk of brass. Pretty soon it got to plaguing the almighty hell out of me—'What's the use in them?' I said to myself. 'They ain't even good to look at.'—and finally one day I couldn't stand the sight of them no more, and I yanked one away from the child and plunked it in the well, but may God take the striffening out of me if my woman don't turn up the next week with another of them popish contraptions! That's the way it went on for a long time, with me snatching off the crosses and plunking them in the well as fast as ever I clapped eyes on them. Last night I was coming back from the barn, and all at once I got the notion to take a peek down in the well,

17

and sure enough, there's all them crosses standing out plain in the light I was flashing down the hole. I got me a spade, and I dumped in some loose sand, and then, b'Josh, I don't see them no more—but, shoot, when I got in the house, there was my woman kneeling down by the bed and praying at a powerful big *wooden* cross! I asked her what she's doing on the floor that time of night, but she kept right on praying, so I laid a good cuff alongside of her jaw. . . . Her and the child cleared out for Vermont on the morning bus, and all the woman left behind was a busted upper plate."

"Good for you, Joel," I said. "You made a convert."

"Two," he said.

HENRY MANSFIELD

b. 1877-

"How's dry-goods and notions, Hank?" I said.

He said, "I come to see you about a dream I been having kind of regular for a good long while now. . . . I'm walking in the woods, and I run across a house I ain't never saw before, and being killing thirsty, I go up to the door and give it a knock. It sort of swings in when I rap it, and I see there ain't nobody living there. The chairs and tables is pretty near all of them turned over, and chips of china is laying around the floor, along with old clothes and rags as hard as shingles. The wall-paper is wound up like flags, and the mirrow on the side-board, you might say, is lacking a front tooth. Halfway out of a cupboard, a mattress is gapping as

18

if it's a tongue, and on the mattress is a old boot. I go to the kitchen, and in a big mixing-bowl that sets under a shelf, I find the skelerton of a mouse. I figure it must of been snooping along the shelf and fell in, and while I'm standing there, I sort of see it happen all over again. It tumbles in, and for a minute it squats in the bottom of the bowl, working its nose and whiskers, and then it tries to creep up to the edge: it only gets so far, and it slides back. It tries again some place else, and the same thing happens. It gets a little excited now and makes a run for it, and after trying that a couple or three times and winding up just where it was in the first place, it goes crazy and takes to running around in circles. It don't never *stop* running. It runs for hours and hours, and maybe other mice look down from the shelf to watch it go nowheres, and after all that time it ain't running so fast, and then it can't hardly drag itself, and finally it stops and keels over and dies. . . . I don't know the people that own the house—like I say, I never seen it in my life—but it comes to me that I got to get busy putting it to rights. I don't know why I feel like that—it just seems natural—so back goes everything where it belongs, and the last thing I do is make a coffin for the mouse out of a old tea-tin and bury it under a tree. I stick my head back in the door to see maybe there's something I forgot, and all in a flash I'm so jumping mad at what I went and done that I have to go inside again and muss up what it took me two hours to smooth down!"

I said, "How long've you had that dry-goods and notion store, Hank?"

"I'm asking you about the dream," he said.

She said, "Every so often, I get a little dizzy in the head."

I said, "Don't wear your corset so tight."

"And sometimes I get a funny kind of a pain right here—thobbing."

"Baking-soda's a nickel a pound."

"I get night-sweats, specially in summer."

"Take a hammer and pull the planking off your windows."

"What should I put on these bramble-scratches?"

"Spit."

"Doc," she said, "I don't feel good. I'm nauseous."

"By God," I said, "I'm beginning to notice it!"

He said, "What's good for a bellyache, Doc?"

I said, "Your wife, Gus—any day in the week."

He said, "And twice on Sunday."

## ANSON UPDEGROVE

### b. 1932-

"Banjo's sick," he said.

"I'm not a dog-doctor, Anse," I said.

"What kind of a doctor are you, then?"

"I'm a doctor for people."

"Dogs are people."

"Anse," I said, "tell Banjo to step in and undress."

## BANJO

### b. 1936-d. 1940

*Distemper.*

## DAVID UPDEGROVE

### b. 1905-

"How's Anse?" I said.

"He ain't so good, Doc," he said. "Ain't been good all spring."

"Come on in here, and I'll give you something to perk him up."

"Since when you keeping your pills in the carriage-house, Doc?"

"Reach down back of that crate."

"Ouch!" he said.

"You damn fool!" I said. "Who told you to take him by the tail?"

"Thanks, you mean-tempered old stinker."

"Clear out, Dave. You're worrying the bitch."

She said, "How much I owe you, Doc?"

I said, "A dollar and a kiss."

"How'll you take it?"

"Well, I'll take the kiss in cash."

"And the dollar?"

"In trade."

"I ought to slap your sassy face, you silly old stud."

"How about four cans of your crab-apple, then?"

"My crab-apple ain't on the market."

"Make it four Damson."

"It's a deal," she said, "but you got to give me twenty cents boot."

"How come, you cut-throat?" I said.

"Four cans of Damson comes to a dollar-twenty."

"Hell, I don't give any boot."

"The deal's off."

"Suppose I throw in six extra pills."

"It's a deal again."

"Now, kiss me that kiss," I said, "and be certain sure you put some teeth in it."

She tipped up her poke, took my face in her hands, and did her best, and it was a good best, but in the end, shaking her head, she looked away. "You should of caught me forty years ago," she said. "I can't kiss with teeth when I only got gums."

## CLEO BEEKMAN (BRANCH)

### b. 1890-

"Steve," she said, "they tell me you've got a patient down to Lake George."

I said, "I've got three-four down there, Cleo."

"A brand-new patient, Steve—a woman-patient, they tell me."

"Who tells you?"

"They say she's a mighty handsome-looking case. They say she needs about one call a week to keep her in shape. Is that true, Steve?"

"Yes, it is," I said.

"Why did you do it, Steve? Wasn't I enough for you?"

"I'm only human, Cleo."

"So am I."

"The woman's gone back to Albany, and it's finished. We oughtn't to let it get in our way."

"I'm human too," she said, "and the next time Jeff comes around to the house, he'll find it out."


## JEFF BRANCH

### b. 1887-

I said, "What're you doing here on this day of all days?"

He said, "I wanted to see you, Doc."

"I could've lived without seeing you."

"I came down to ask if you wouldn't shake hands and say there's no hard feelings."

"Go put on your hard collar and slick down your hair: you'll be late for the only wedding I ever wanted to go to."

"I never worked you any harm, Steve."

"The hell you say!"

"You've got something against me, and I wish to God I knew what it was."

"God's out to lunch."

"Well, I've been on my hands and knees long enough," he said, but he looked back from the doorway. "Cleo's going to feel bad about you not unwinding any."

"I'm only human," I said. "I'm only human, do you hear? Say to Miss Cleo Beekman that I'm only human!"

"I will, Doc," he said, and the door was closed.

## MISS FINCH

### b. 1896-

"Doc," she said, "I asked you over to take a look at the new girl I got from the Poor Home. I don't want nobody working for me that ain't sound in wind and limb."

I said, "Bring the horse in."

"Come here, Lizzie," she said.

b. 1925-

I said, "What did they teach you at the Poor Home, Liz?"

"Prayers," she said.

"Recite me one of them."

" 'In love and wisdom hast Thou, O God, apportioned the lot of all Thy creatures, and we must accept with resignation whatever position Thy providence hath assigned to us, and endeavor to fulfil faithfully all the duties incident thereto. . . .' "

"Now, there's a prayer that weighs a pound and a half!" I said.

"It ain't done yet," she said. " '. . . Inspire me, therefore, with a proper understanding so that I may not fail in comprehending the obligations required of me as subordinate to the will of others, and so that I may obtain Thy favor and the good will of those who are placed above me.' "

"Honey," I said, "do you know what all that means?"

"Sure," she said. "It means I'm supposed to keep my trap shut and sweat like a stone crock."

I went to the door and called Miss Finch. "Miss Finch," I said, "you got stuck. I find that Liz has glanders and spavin, in addition to which she's blind in the off-eye," and taking the girl by the arm, I marched her out to the road, saying, "Liz, before I show you down to my house, how'd you like a chocolate soda?"

"Make it strawberry, Doc!" she said. "Please, Doc, please make it strawberry! I been wanting one for five years . . . !"

## DECKY LOMAX
### b. 1934-

I said, "Christmas Eve is no time for a little girl to be sick."

She said, "I wouldn't of got nothing, anyway."

"Don't you believe in Santa Claus?"

"No."

"Would you believe in him if you woke up tomorrow morning and found a silver dollar under your pillow?"

"No," she said. "I'd believe in you."

## MARK LOMAX
### b. 1900-

I said, "Why'd you beat on her like that, Mark?"

"I was learning her to fear the Lord," he said.

"You'll kill her some day."

"I believe in Jesus Christ!"

## DANIEL HUNTER
### b. 1904-

I said, "Dan, do you believe in Santa Claus?"

He said, "No, but I believe in children."

26

"Doc," he said, "I want a penny's worth of castor-oil."

I said, "Big, a penny's worth of castor-oil wouldn't physic a frog."

"Don't know any frogs," he said, and taking a cent from his pocket, he spun it on the glass top of my desk and watched it till the spin petered out and the coin chattered down.

I said, "You Indians are the only Americans that shy away from gab."

"I want to swab out the barrels of my over-and-under."

"You fixing to burn up some powder?"

"Partridge."

"It's four weeks too early for partridge."

"What's that orange button on your vest, Doc?"

"A hunting-button, same as the one on your hat-band."

"I wear mine all the time."

"Me too," I said, "and you know why? Because shooting's about the best fun there is."

"Sometimes I can't hardly wait for the seasons to open."

"Having Game Laws is a pretty smart idea, though," I said. "Where'd all the game be if a man could go banging away any time of the year?"

"Hard to tell," he said.

"Easy to tell," I said. "Inside of a year, there wouldn't be anything left to shoot at but people."

"That's why I say sometimes I can't hardly wait."

"Of course, Big," I said, "I'm not trying to make out I never broke the law. I can remember when I didn't pay much attention to it. I kept on forgetting all the time."

"Funny thing," he said. "That use to happen to me."

"Even now, I kind of lose track every once in a while."

"You know, Steve," he said, "you ask me, I think the two of us is just a pair of common poachers."

### CLARA PENROSE

### b. 1902-

She said, "What kind of a trip did you have in New York, Doc?"

"Pretty good, Clara," I said.

"I met a feller from New York this summer. Met him at a dance. He said he was in the jewelry business, and I guess he was telling the truth because he shown me pictures of the stuff he sells. Some of it was awful pretty—specially the rings."

"What kind of rings, Clara?"

"Oh, all kinds. The wedding-rings was pretty as any."

"What did you want to see me about?"

"The man's name was Thomas."

"That's a good name."

28

"You didn't happen to run across a man name of Thomas when you was in New York, did you, Doc?"

"Thomas? Thomas? No, I don't think I did, Clara. What was his first name?"

"*That* was his first name. I never did find out the other."

"Was there anything particular you wanted to see me about, Clara?"

"I guess not, Doc," she said.

### ABRAHAM NOVINSKY

#### b. 1879-

". . . It happened in the Old Country a long time ago," he said. "I was only a boy. . . . All day the people of the village had been working in the fields, and now it was late, and the sun was going down, and the air was so still that even over the little hills you could hear the scythes whispering through the grain, as if they were talking to each other. It was pleasant in the fields. It was very peaceful. . . . And then, in one heart-beat, the calm was gone. The Soldiers came, a mile-long curve of horsemen, a scythe that let the grain stand and cut the people down. We ran, but the river stopped us, and in a moment we were surrounded. The Officer ordered all the unmarried women to come forth, and eight girls obeyed him, standing close together in a little sheaf. The Officer ordered them to take off their clothes and climb into the trees along the river-bank, but this time they made no move. The

Officer cried, '*Take off your clothes, I said! Take off your clothes!*' I watched my sister. I watched her loosen her skirt and blouse and drop them to the ground; I saw her naked body, and I still remember how very beautiful it was. '*Now, get up into those trees and sing like birds!*' the Officer said, and after the girls had climbed in among the leaves, he waited for the song. Only the sound of weeping came from the trees. '*Climb higher!*' he shouted; '*Climb higher and sing like birds!*' The trees came to life as the girls worked their way up toward the top branches. A thin little song came floating down, and then many thin little songs, and all of them together were hardly enough to reach the ground. The Officer shook his head. '*No more singing,*' he said; '*It's too sad. I want to see you fly now. I want to see you fly like birds!*' Not knowing what to do, the girls began to flap their arms. '*That's not good enough,*' the Officer said; '*That's not flying at all,*' and turning to the Soldiers, he gave a command: '*Make those cows fly like birds!*' The Soldiers raised their rifles and fired into the trees. The bodies of eight naked girls tumbled from the branches and fell into the river. '*They flew!*' the Officer cried; '*They flew just like birds!*' And then he galloped his horse away across the fields, and the Soldiers followed him, and in a few moments the late afternoon was quiet once more. . . ."

"Abe," I said, "why do you come to our church?"

"Sometimes I like to pray," he said, "and in Warrensburg I have no place of my own."

"But when you think of your sister. . . ."

30

"That's when I like to pray," he said. "That's when I come to your church."

## THOMAS LIGGETT PAULHAN

### b. 1899-d. 1939

*He said, ". . . She came out toward the middle of the dance-floor—not walking, not just walking, but flowing like a breaker—and slowly she began to flirt the carnation of her dress, a dozen knee-high skirts amber-swirling, and slowly she played them with her hips, and still slowly she played them with her groin, and then—and always faster, and now with her head too, and her hair, and her clubbing breasts—she played* herself, *and finally the skirts came to a boil, and in her hands the wooden shells stuttered like drum-fire as she tried to throw her fingers away, and again and again she pounded her heels and always harder, and long gray combs of dust sprang from between the floorboards, and then the music slashed up to one last tearing jerking tin-can smash, the woman's body cake-walking in the after-twitches of a mechanical jigger running down. And it was over. . . ."*

## AARON PLATT

### b. 1900-

I said, "Gracie Paulhan tells me you didn't show up with your dollar last Saturday night."

31

"I had a head-cold," he said, "and I figured she might get it."

"Very considerate of you. You should've done as much for her late husband."

"God damn her late husband!"

"He was God damned when he was alive."

"Me and God don't speak."

"God isn't such a horse-thief when you get to know Him," I said. "He'd have helped you out of that hole if you'd given Him a chance. Tom Paulhan couldn't have lived out that winter with a whole new set of gears. But, no—you had to play God and let the poor bastard die without lifting a finger to hold him back. And then you expect his wife to understand! Where was your sense, Aaron?"

"Never had any far's Tom Paulhan was concerned," he said. "I only knew one thing that morning I found him laying in my barn: he was sick, cold, and starving, and what he was going to get off of me could of been hid behind a hair. He was all done, Doc: I wanted him to die, and I *let* him die, and it wasn't only account of him being married to Grace and bragging about putting the boots to that dance-hall whoor. A man's like a flea; he ain't so particular about the dog he's on. What got my back up was that Tom was *never* any good— from end to end and against the grain. He was all punk except the bark, and the bark's what he'd been trading on right up to the time he laid down in that stall: he didn't know it, but for once he was going to come out the little end of the horn. I was better than him at

32

anything a man can do on his feet, on his hams, on his knees, or on his belly—but he got Grace, and I got a tall tight skinny frump with legs as cold as pipe-iron and a build onto her like a hay-tedder. I should of had his Grace, and he should of had my stiff ice-house beef, with flabby little tits that hung off of her like pockets turned inside-out. I had five years of that, Doc—*five years*—and all the time I was thinking of Grace Tennent Paulhan! Every day Grace! every night Grace! all that live-long buggered-up time—*Grace!* . . . . Let him die? You can lay God odds I did!"

GRACE TENNENT PAULHAN

b. 1902-

She said, "Doc, for years now, you've been coming up here night after night with that syringe. You've never taken any money, and you've never offered any money. . . . Why?"

I said, "For one reason, Gracie—to hear you ask that question."

"Well," she said, "I've asked it."

"I come every night with this syringe," I said, "because I know that Aaron Platt comes every Saturday night with his dollar."

"He'll always get his money's worth."

"I want him to get more."

"He never will, Doc."

"The way Tom died—is it still that?"

She lay there naked, her arms at her sides, her fingers

33

picking at the candlewicks on the coverlet. I sat in a chair next to the bed, and I remember that as I repeated the question, I was looking at the trade-name and patent-number of the syringe.

"Is it still that, Gracie?" I said. "Do I still have to tell Aaron he's only a customer?"

"Tell him, Doc . . . ," she said, and suddenly she was a young girl again, and crying very quietly, ". . . tell him. . . . I think he's getting to be a friend."

✿

The church was silent now: no shoes scraped, and no voices whispered. Reaching out over the pulpit with his palms turned up in invitation, Hunter addressed the assembly.

"Brothers . . . ," he said.

✿

# AT POLK'S STORE

WHEN the door was opened, the wind came in, and with the wind the cold spring rain. The smoke in the air, disturbed, was baled like hay, and from wall to wall the shadow of a hanging lamp seesawed in syncopation. And then the door was closed and the wet wind shut out, and as the smoke expanded, slowly the lamp ran down and hung still. Drops of water descended the woman's coat, clung for an instant to the fibres of the hem, glistening, and fell to the floor.

"You want anything, nigger?" Behind one of the counters, Leland Polk was jacked up on his elbows between two tin-can pyramids.

"Is this your store?" the woman said.

"The name is Polk."

"I just walked up from Lake George," the woman said.

Near Polk's head, a spiral of fly-paper drilled the smoke-marbled air.

"It's raining," the woman said.

"The name is Polk, nigger."

"Do you mind if I dry off a little?"

"The name is Polk!"

"I only wan᷑ to sit by the stove," the woman said.

*"Mister Polk!"*

In the pause, a clock went into the convulsion of labor; a litter of eight strokes was born.

"You can keep right on walking," Polk said.

"Let her stay, Leland," Bishop said. The words were spoken from the mezzanine of darkness outside the light-cone. Crossed at the ankles, a pair of disembodied legs swung gently below the counter opposite Polk. "Let her stay."

"Butt out, Eli," Polk said.

"You don't want us to get a bad name, do you?"

"Who's us?"

"Town of Warrensburg," Bishop said.

"Since when's the town keeping my store?"

"I didn't say it was keeping your store."

"A man don't want the town smelling around his business," Polk said, "and don't ever think he does."

"Anybody smelled around me, I'd be mad," Bishop said.

"A store's property, and it belongs to the man that owns it—lock, stock, and barrel."

"Christ Himself couldn't beat him out of it."

"And if the town don't like his ways, that's just too God damn bad for the town."

Bishop blew a squid of smoke down from the shadow,

36

and it wrapped itself around his swinging legs. "All the same, Leland," he said, "a man's got a duty."

"A duty?" Polk said. "What kind of a duty?"

"A duty to keep up the town's character."

"Never knew a town *had* a character."

"Take a town like Riparius," Bishop said. "Supposing a man come up to you and said, 'Leland, what kind of a place is Riparius?' You'd tell him straight out, 'Riparius? Why, man, that town's prettier than a little red pair of shoes!'"

The clock clenched for an after-birth of a single stroke.

"Warrensburg's a different kind of a hairpin," Polk said.

"That's a God-Almighty fact, Leland, but it's got a character all the same."

"You know what I'd tell that man about Warrensburg?" Polk said. "I'd say, 'Mister, Warrensburg's as tight as a deacon's drawers.'"

"That's the first time I ever heard a complain," Bishop said. "You don't talk to enough people, Leland. You're cooped up too much."

"Don't ever think I ain't," Polk said.

"You ask me, I'd say Warrensburg's a *friendly* town."

"The only fresh air I get is when a customer comes in and sneezes."

"I kind of take pride in Warrensburg," Bishop said.

"I don't get any more sunshine than a clam."

37

"Yes, sir," Bishop said, "I kind of take pride in it—and that's why I wouldn't turn nobody out in the rain."

"I take pride in the town myself, Eli."

"Then you got to be friendly to strangers."

"It don't pay to be *too* friendly," Polk said.

"You got to show them the character of the town."

"A man can be *too* friendly, and don't ever think he can't."

"If you ain't fixed so's you can be ho*spit*able," Bishop said, "you got to recommend somebody that is."

"Suppose *you* make a recommend, Eli," Polk said.

"What about the Adirondack Inn?"

"Not open yet."

"The Secor House."

"Full up."

Bishop let himself down off the counter, and for a moment he stood studying the red and gold band around the stub of his cigar. "I guess that only leaves the boarding-house, then," he said, and looking full at Polk, he licked a loose leaf of tobacco.

"Boarding-house?" Polk said. "What boarding-house?"

"Did you say you was born in Warrensburg, Leland?"

"Born upstairs, and don't ever think I wasn't."

"Then you ought to know the town pretty good."

"Mister, I know it up, down, and slaunchways."

"Up and down, maybe, but not slaunchways," Bishop said. "Gracie Paulhan takes boarders, Leland."

The storekeeper stared at him through the languid

38

smoke, and then, grinning, he said, "Now, that's the God-Al*might*iest fact, Eli."

✿

## AT GRACE PAULHAN'S

Rainwater pools were spittoons for rain, the throats of gutters gargled rain, eavesdrop dripped like broken beads, and rain, for leaves, was a slap in the face: the night moved in rain, falling, filling, brimming over, and wandering.

The faint figure of a man, his pajama-shirt shoved into his pants, blocked the faint crack of the partly open door. "*Boarding*-house?" he said.

"That's what they told me," the woman said.

"They must of been codding you, ma'am."

"This isn't a boarding-house, then?"

"Not the kind you're looking for, ma'am."

In a room off the parlor, a bed-spring sprang. "Who is she, Aaron?" Grace said.

"Somebody they was codding down to Polk's."

"Tell her to come in."

Behind the mica features of a stove glowed the remnants of a fire; now and then, as the coals unfurled pennants of flame, the pumpkin face expressed surprise. There was warmth in the house, a warmth that bunted the stranger like sleep.

Grace came into the parlor wearing a cotton wrapper over her cotton night-gown. "My name is Grace Paulhan," she said.

"Glad to know you," the woman said.

"And this is Aaron Platt, a friend of mine."

"Please to meet you," Platt said, "but you might as well know right off that Leland Polk's the kind of a man that I wouldn't help him if he was kicking in a ditch."

"Where'd you come from, miss?" Grace said.

"Down the road a ways."

"And Eli Bishop," Platt said, "he thinks he's something on a stick."

"Do you know anyone in Warrensburg?" Grace said.

"No," the woman said.

"The whole damn town," Platt said, "there's only a screen-door between it and hell's backside."

"Aaron!"

"Excuse the expression, Gracie."

Grace put her hand on the woman's arm. "I wish I could ask you to stay here," she said.

"I'm sorry I troubled you this hour of night," the woman said, and, turning, she opened the door.

A wind had come to police the crowd of rain: broken, it fled drumming down the roof, it beat a tick-tack-toe on the tin gutters, and it dove into the marsh of lawn and disappeared.

"Can't we fix you something to eat?" Grace said.

The woman shook her head and waded away up the path, a gravel shallow in the submerged grass. There were night-sounds now in the dwindling rain: leaves saying *leaves, leaves*; the amusement of water among stones; the stuttered utterance of swaying wood; and, run through once, the wood-wind music of a distant thrush.

40

Grace leaned against the door-jamb, listening to foot-steps going. "Aaron . . . ," she said.

"Ma'am."

"Take her up to Dan's."

"Dan who?"

"Dan won't turn her out."

"Dan Hunter?"

"Yes," she said.

"If the town ever seen that woman up to the par-sonage, Dan'd have to find himself a round church so's the Devil couldn't corner him."

"Dan isn't afraid of the Devil."

"And the town ain't afraid of *God*. They'd run Dan so bow-legged he couldn't stop a hog in a hallway."

"I let that woman go away empty-handed, Aaron. . . ."

"She ain't none of your lookout."

". . . And I can do the same to you."

"You're getting your tail over a line for nothing, Gracie."

"I wouldn't want to send you home so early," she said. "I look forward all week to Saturday night."

"Grace . . . ," he said, and the whispered word was silk on silk.

"Yes, Aaron?"

"If I take her up there, can I come back for the same dollar?"

"Yes, Aaron," she said.

✿

Driving a horse harnessed outside its blanket, Platt overtook the woman near the far side of Thurman bridge. He reined in.

"She sent me after you, ma'am."

"I didn't ask for charity," the woman said.

"You give me a chase," he said. "I figured you went back towards town."

"You only go back when you're ready to beg."

"Climb up, ma'am."

"Where are we going?"

"Climb up," he said. "It ain't far."

The side-road to Number Four Pond was a brook now that ran downhill along the interlocking fingers of a rail-fence. The wagon walked the waterway on spokes.

"I didn't catch the name, ma'am," Platt said.

Trees laid wet hands upon them from the roadside. The woman grasped one that detained her and stripped it clean. From her fist grew a rose of leaves.

"You take Dan Hunter, now . . . ," Platt said.

And with the stopping rain, the night-time stalk began, the stalk of food stalking food in the bread-line of the forest. The chain—water to earth to air to fire—was silently forming in the damp darkness, and the frog lived only for the snake, the snake for the hawk, the hawk for the spring-gun in the barnyard.

". . . He ain't no God damn Leland Polk."

At the edge of a pond, on the dry palm of a water-lily, a frog sat waiting to wrap its tangle-foot tongue around a moth. A yard away and motionless, a grass-snake blended with its cover—green body for green grass, yellow bib for wild mustard. Overhead, the branches of a beech rose and fell on a groundswell of wind, and rising and falling with one of them were the sulphur feet of a sharp-shinned hawk. One mile off, on the fence of a chicken-run, a red and round cardboard maggot lay deep in a long steel tube.

"He's a white man, Dan is," Platt said.

In the distance, a single shot was fired, the sound coming downwind diminished, like the chug of an axe.

"Excuse the expression, ma'am."

"That's all right," the woman said.

Under a nap of mist, the Pond lay in the lap of a seated hill. Beyond, hanging against its chest like a lavaliere, was a small white church.

"Dan's place," Platt said.

As the wagon neared the parsonage, an oblong hole of light broke the dark. Pasted in the door-frame was the cut-out of a man.

"Hi, Dan," Platt said.

"Who's there?" Hunter said.

"Me—Aaron Platt."

"A hell of a time to come to church."

"Any time's a hell of a time."

"You're half a day early for a sermon."

"Early! I'm six and a half days late."

"Who've you got with you?"

43

"Somebody they told her Grace ran a boarding-house."

"Who told her?"

"Couple of your pew-holders."

"Named . . . ?"

"How many you got in your congregation, Dan?"

"Forty-odd. Why?"

"Hold your nose and take your choice."

"Come on in and have a cup of coffee," Hunter said. "You too, miss."

The woman started to climb down, but with one foot on the step, she caved in like clothes fallen from a hanger. Hunter tried to catch her as she sagged.

"Get Doc Slocum, Aaron," Hunter said as he carried her into the parsonage. "And stop off for Gracie."

✿

## "I'LL BRING YOU BACK CHICAGO"

### 1492 A.D.

FRIDAY, 3RD OF AUGUST

We sailed from Palos at eight in the morning,
and heading southwest with a five-mile breeze,
we held our course till the sun went under,
and the land was lost in the port-side night:
we were on our way to the Canaries and Japan.

SATURDAY, 4TH OF AUGUST

We corrected southwest by a quarter south.

SUNDAY, 5TH OF AUGUST

The wind held good the whole day and night,
and we reeled off a hundred and twenty miles.

MONDAY, 6TH OF AUGUST

The day's run was ninety miles, give or take,
and we'd have doubled it, maybe tripled it,
if the *Pinta* hadn't balked in the afternoon.

45

She unshipped her rudder and went like a crab,
walked sideways on the water, venting wind,
wasted a day-long bellyful of westbound wind,
and we wasted it too—naked and dawdling—
while bums fumbled with her dragging tail.
Christ only knows how it came out of joint,
Christ . . . ? Or does Rascon know, or Quintero?
They bulged their pants in dread of the voyage,
and having come, now they bilge up the ship.

TUESDAY, 7TH OF AUGUST
Day and night, we made seventy-five miles.

WEDNESDAY, 8TH OF AUGUST
A sea-going curse on Rascon and Quintero
for teaching the *Pinta* their infant tricks:
she too makes water; she too fills her pants.

SUNDAY, 12TH OF AUGUST
Three limping days, and it's the Canaries.

WEDNESDAY, 5TH OF SEPTEMBER
The crews are brave again and big with brag:
a month on land to forget the water future,
and in work and wine they've forgotten it,
forgotten it or faked it till the day came.
Well, the day's here, you marinated pirates,
and you ride with the tide in the morning—
you ride, or you rot with some island quean
while we make the Indies or drown in salt.
Name your poison, you pickled buccaneers!

46

THURSDAY, 6TH OF SEPTEMBER
The ebb drained us out of the Gomera roads
as if a bung had been started in the ocean,
and between us and gold lay an arc of water,
but the wind was a sigh from a tired old man,
and all day we heard laughter on the beach.
Damn God for pooping out when we needed Him!
What's He think we're doing here—fishing?

FRIDAY, 7TH OF SEPTEMBER
They swam out to us today, still laughing,
they prodded the dead air with dirty jokes,
and they swam back, kicking up a galling wake:
the crews were much amused by the horse-play.

SATURDAY, 8TH OF SEPTEMBER
A northeaster caught hold after sundown,
driving us twenty-seven miles by midnight:
we took in a strangling sea over the bows.

SUNDAY, 9TH OF SEPTEMBER
We made a cool hundred and forty-seven miles,
and during the day's run, we lost the earth.
The crews whined as it settled under water,
shed tears of fear, and spoke of turning back:
we'll turn back, men—when I'm    od for fish
or they for me on cutlery of hammered gold.

MONDAY, 10TH OF SEPTEMBER
The steering today stank up the Atlantic:
our course was west, but the whole day long

we yawed off to the north or south of it,
the fancy needlework costing us a solid run.
Even so, we made a hundred and eighty miles,
but now the watches tumble in their sleep,
and blood runs deep in their mumbled mutiny.

TUESDAY, 11TH OF SEPTEMBER
The men got a bargain rate of speed today:
we sailed due west a hundred and twenty miles,
but knocked off a dozen to sweeten the price.

WEDNESDAY, 12TH OF SEPTEMBER
Day and night, we covered a flat one hundred,
but for the quaking crews it was eighty-five.

THURSDAY, 13TH OF SEPTEMBER
All day the wind was like a running brook,
all day the canvas boomed and lured us west.
We ran four miles to the hour, an even four,
but faked it to lay a ghost at nightfall,
when the needle and north parted company.

FRIDAY, 14TH OF SEPTEMBER
We had a sign, a sign of birds in the Flood!
The *Niña* saw a *rabo de junco*, the reedtail,
and later a *garjao*, the swallow of the sea,
and when the lying words (my own) took wing—
that these were birds that hugged the land—
the men fell down and foamed at the mouth.
A sign? Now, how in holy hell would *I* know?
Did I ever watch the habits of the royal tern?
We made sixty miles, counting fifty for fools.

SATURDAY, 15TH OF SEPTEMBER
We ran ninety miles, but I reported less:
a flame from Heaven plunged into the sea,
and we had fireworks all night—below deck.

SUNDAY, 16TH OF SEPTEMBER
There were some clouds and a small rain,
and running a hundred and seventeen miles,
we palmed nine to keep the men sanitary.
They saw bright green tufts of grass today,
and they rejoiced, saying that land was near,
maybe even the Indies, or, Christ, Japan!
Let them rave: if there's anything but water,
if there's land within a thousand miles of us,
may God stuff me full of it, piece by piece!

MONDAY, 17TH OF SEPTEMBER
Again there was grass, and herbs from rocks,
and among the herbs a living thing, a crab.
Tunny-fish were seen, and a boatswain-bird,
and the men drew up a bucket of sea-water,
and, tonguing it, found it to be less salt.
I sampled it myself, and it'd pickle herring.
The run today was a hundred and fifty miles,
but the men got ten off for good behavior.

TUESDAY, 18TH OF SEPTEMBER
The *Pinta* (Mr. Pinzon) spoke us at noon:
a fleet of birds had overhauled the ship
and tumbled west, dead ahead, toward home,
and being the crack sailer of the outfit,

she was on tip-toe to follow their flight,
to push on and be first to make a landfall.
Go, I said, and she was away from the mark
as if she'd outrun the sun to the horizon.
We made good a hundred and sixty-five miles
and caught the *Pinta* dogging it after dark.

WEDNESDAY, 19TH OF SEPTEMBER
We had a fine-grained rain and so little wind
that flying all our canvas, even our drawers,
we bagged enough for only seventy-five miles.
An *alcatraz*, the booby-bird, landed on deck,
and the men had a sign, a sign from the sky:
they grieved when the sign got sick and puked.

THURSDAY, 20TH OF SEPTEMBER
This was a day on wings, a day of birds:
two boobies found us out among the weeds,
and a third, and then a bird we took by hand,
a swimmer, a river-bird with mittened feet,
and land-birds, two or three, came singing,
and again, at evening, a second *alcatraz*.
We plodded twenty miles through the swamp.

FRIDAY, 21ST OF SEPTEMBER
We didn't have to fake the forty-mile run,
for there was no wind: there was only weed,
and the fleet sailed it like toys on a lawn.
A whale came up veiled, its veil of grass,
and the sea breathed slowly in its sleep.

50

SATURDAY, 22ND OF SEPTEMBER
The sailors had the trots for ninety miles:
the wind was all *from* Spain, never *toward* it,
the wind was on the tail, never in the face,
the wind was a one-way wind, a way unknown.
It's too bad they were so drizzling scared;
it's too bad they cocked no eye at birds:
they missed a new one today—the petrel.

SUNDAY, 23RD OF SEPTEMBER
The men were even looser in the morning:
they ran front and rear now, babbling wind
I'd have given an arm to catch with canvas.
We were good for sixty-six miles, drifting.

MONDAY, 24TH OF SEPTEMBER
A strong swimmer would've lost us today:
we cruised a mile and a half to the hour
and got beat by the crabs, even by the weed.
We'll make tracks at dawn, or I'm a liar;
we'll sail, b'Jesus, or we'll walk on water:
nobody sits and picks his nose in this outfit.

TUESDAY, 25TH OF SEPTEMBER
We walked this day—not on water, but air.
Land was sighted when the sun went down!
Land, a long low wreck with its decks awash!
Land, a crack in the seam of sea and sky!
Land! Do you understand? We sighted land!
Mr. Pinzon (the *Pinta*) thanked God, kneeling,
and said the *Gloria* for his kneeling crew,

and on the *Niña* they shinnied up the masts
for a bird's-eye view of the island of Japan.
Land, a reef of it at seventy-five miles!
On the flagship, though, it was half and half:
we prayed a little, and we rubbered a little—
it might've been land, but it wasn't Japan.

WEDNESDAY, 26TH OF SEPTEMBER
There was land at dawn, but two miles down:
nothing, not even a bird, rode the empty ocean
when the sun came up and blood-shot the day.
It must've been a cloud they saw, and it sank.
From now on, I've got my back to the wall:
the men are quiet, but knives have tongues.

THURSDAY, 27TH OF SEPTEMBER
We made seventy miles, but counted sixty,
and the men took it staring, saying nothing,
and when the *dorados* came, the gilded fish,
they killed them quietly, as if for practice.

FRIDAY, 28TH OF SEPTEMBER
The Ark would've given us a brush today:
we had little weed, less wind, and no talk,
and running forty miles, we counted the same.

SATURDAY, 29TH OF SEPTEMBER
A pair of boobies dozed in the shrouds,
loaded with garbage and dead to the world,
and being heavy-laden, being booby-galleons
with a cargo of food imported from Spain,

they were prize pickings, they were fair game
for the frigate-bird, the fork-tailed pirate,
and falling on them, he ran them so dizzy
they shot him a meal that he took on the fly.
The crews too opened their mouths today:
seventy-two miles shrank to sixty-three,
yet the talk was of wind and water-weed.

SUNDAY, 30TH OF SEPTEMBER
I gave thirty-three miles for forty-two:
if we ever get home, I'll confess it some day.

MONDAY, 1ST OF OCTOBER
A fair run, with some heavy showers of rain:
we put a good seventy-five miles behind us,
but the count stopped at sixty for the crew.

TUESDAY, 2ND OF OCTOBER
The weed drifts now from the east to the west,
as if we were in a river flowing to Japan,
and we had a run today worthy of the name—
a downstream hundred and seventeen miles:
I threw them ninety, and they swallowed it.

WEDNESDAY, 3RD OF OCTOBER
They must've been abused in their dreams,
or self-abused, and they ran me ragged today:
they wanted me to give up the straight course,
they wanted me to hemstitch north and south,
they wanted me to make a dog-leg every watch.
I told them to go back to sleep and to hell,

but they stayed on deck, and they stayed awake,
and it was even-money I wouldn't last the day
without pulling another rabbit out of my hat.
It would've been hard to die needing a sign,
and if God knew it, it was He that sent one:
weed—some old, some fresh and wearing fruit.
I took twenty miles off the hundred and forty,
but it was the weed that saved me for history.

THURSDAY, 4TH OF OCTOBER
We ran for the record today, and broke it:
we ran a hundred and ninety miles, but broke it,
cut it to a hundred and forty for the people.
Item: a ship's boy struck a booby with a stone.

FRIDAY, 5TH OF OCTOBER
Again the ships were red-hot in the keel,
and again we burned grooves in the water:
we made good a hundred and seventy-one miles,
but somehow or other we were three dozen shy
when the men came aft to learn our position.
Many thanks be to God for the temperate air,
and for the day's miracle, the flying-fish
that came up from the sea to walk the plank.

SATURDAY, 6TH OF OCTOBER
Mr. Pinzon put in his two cents again today:
it'd be wise, he said, to sail west by south,
to forget the continent and make for Japan;
take Japan, he said, and let the Indies go.
If he tries that song again before we land,

he'll find himself singing it from both ends:
while I'm the Admiral, I'll set the course,
and while Pinzon's under me, he'll follow it.
We were good for a hundred and twenty miles,
but I pruned twenty-one for double figures.

SUNDAY, 7TH OF OCTOBER
Day and night they've searched for signs—
they've sought them in the flight of birds,
in the uncommon fish and the berried weed,
in the hue of the water, in the sounding-lead,
in the composition of the sea-bottom sand,
in the rain and the wind and the log-line lies:
day and night they've hunted clues to land,
and all God could give to sailors, they've had—
or almost all, for they've never had the dream.
It was an Admiral's dream, and I dreamed it
for the first time when I first saw a ship,
and again, and always, when I walked on wood,
and when I spun the hearsay globes of scholars,
and once more the first night out from Palos.
Since then, nothing in the dark but the wind,
till last night, nothing—and again the dream,
but now no longer hope, but mineral and real,
and when morning broke, dust was in my mouth,
and knowing we'd reached the promised land,
I put a little something to the Crown reward,
a silk doublet for him with the sharpest eye—
and we were top-heavy with men in the rigging.

The day-and-night run was eighty-four miles,
but thirty came off to keep us nearer Spain.

MONDAY, 8TH OF OCTOBER
The sea today was like the river at Seville,
and we idled down it for thirty-six miles.

TUESDAY, 9TH OF OCTOBER
We made ninety miles and counted but fifty:
all night long there were birds passing by.

WEDNESDAY, 10TH OF OCTOBER
When the day opened with water to the rim,
when I saw the sea a circle vacant to the sky,
I wondered how much longer I had to breathe.
The men told me, and I took their word for it:
three days, they gave me, three whole days
to say my prayers for some ground to pray on,
and if, they said, no land was then in sight,
they were going back—with me or without me.
We made a hundred and seventy-seven miles,
but I slashed it to a hundred and forty-two:
a hell of a day God picked to give us wind!

THURSDAY, 11TH OF OCTOBER
We ran off a hundred and fifty miles today,
and I sighted land at ten in the evening.
Item: don't forget to claim the reward.

☼

# AT THE POST OFFICE

THE MORNING sun hit the fretwork of the porch and broke itself into flinders of light, each one mobile with cinders and turning dust. Near the ceiling, a traffic of green flies skidded on the splintered air.

"What's her name, Doc?" Bishop said.

In the warming day, several townsmen were waiting for the first mail from Lake George, some on the jigsaw railing, some in chairs tilted against the wall, and one, Doc Slocum, on the steps leading to the road.

Bishop blew a tadpole of foaming spit over the railing and watched it ball up in the dirt. "Doc," he said, "what's the nigger's name?"

Slocum leaned back against the banister and looked up at a dried leak in the ceiling, a geodetic stain charting the topography of an unfamiliar country. A fly rowed upside-down across a body of wooden water, and reaching an electric-wire, it fell into the air and flew away.

"If she's a nigger," Hustis said, "what the hell's the difference what her name is?"

"She's a nigger, all right," Polk said, "and don't ever think she ain't."

"A name could make all the difference in the world." Bishop said.

"Not to a nigger," Hustis said. "You want them, you just wag your thumb; they don't come, you beat on them with a stout stick."

"A name's a lot more than a way to call a person." Bishop said.

"Far's I'm concerned, everybody's name could be Joe."

"A name tells you who the person is."

"If the person's a nigger, I ain't asking."

"A man's got a right to know strangers."

"He's got a right to drownd himself too, only I never seen him fight for it."

Confrey tugged at a thong that dove into a pocket of his overalls; it emerged dragging a fat watch. "Albany train must of jumped the track," he said.

"She don't go that fast," Smead said.

"Don't ever think she don't," Polk said.

"Ever been to Albany, Leland?" Smead said.

"Once."

"When was that?"

"Close onto thirty years ago."

"Traveled by the cars, I suppose."

"Traveled by wagon," Polk said, "and don't ever think I didn't."

Perched on the face of a sunflower near the porch, a phoebe watched the carousel of flies. It took off, struck, and missed, and the flies continued to wheel in their endless pursuit under the ceiling.

"You don't see many of them around here," Bishop said.

"Many what?" Harned said. "Fly-catchers?"

"Many niggers."

"That Albany train goes fast when she's standing still," Polk said.

"I seen one last summer," Harned said.

"Where at?" Bishop said.

"Front of the Adirondack Inn. He was in a otto*mo*bile."

"A otto*mo*bile!"

"A otto*mo*bile."

"Since when they boarding niggers at the Inn?"

"Nobody said they was."

"You're another, Ash."

"I ain't fine-haired," Harned said, "but I don't like being called a liar right on top of my pancakes. Never did."

"Then don't counterdict yourself," Bishop said.

"I didn't counterdict myself."

"First you said they was putting niggers up at the Inn, and then you said they wasn't. That's counterdictory."

"I only said I seen one setting out front in a otto*mo*bile."

"Then they was boarding him, wasn't they?"

"That don't follow, Eli," Mansfield said.

"He might of just been waiting," Hustis said.

"Now, what would a nigger be waiting for?" Bishop said.

"He might be waiting to wake up."

"I asked a question: What would a nigger be waiting for front of the Inn?"

"Maybe he run out of gas," Piper said.

"Maybe he was ducking the Confederates," Confrey said.

"He picked out a hell of a place, then," Slocum said. "He'd have been safer thumbing his nose at Robert E. Lee than saying 'Mister' to any of you Adirondack copperhead sons-of-bitches."

"I ain't been answered yet," Bishop said. "What was that nigger doing in that otto*m*obile?"

"I know one thing he *wasn't* doing, Eli," Slocum said.

"What's that, Doc?"

"Making a horse's ass of himself."

"I ain't any horse's ass, Doc."

"Well, you're sure doing the work of one."

"I said this before, and I'll say it again: a man's got a right to find out about strangers."

"I never saw it in the Constitution."

"There's lots of things ain't in the Constitution that ought to be."

"For instance, what?"

"For instance, the right to ask a ordinary question."

"Like 'What's a nigger doing in a otto*m*obile?' "

60

"Now, that's a good example, Doc."

"Eli, you're messing up this town worse than a hog's breakfast, and for nothing at all—nothing!"

"A nigger-stranger ain't nothing."

"He's nothing to *me*," Slocum said. "If a man wants to sit in an automobile, I'm for letting him sit there till he starts to decompose."

"He's nothing to me, either, but I got a right to be curious."

"And the woman up at Dan Hunter's?"

"I got a right to be curious about her too."

"I don't see anybody else being curious."

"They got a right *not* to be curious."

"Honest," Slocum said, "I don't know why I use my mouth for anything but eating."

Again the phoebe stooped, and again it missed, but recovering in the air, it struck from a hover, and one of the green flies was missing from the circuit.

"You wouldn't be *hiding* the woman's name, would you, Doc?"

"You can't hide what you don't know."

"You sure you don't know? Just stop and think, Doc."

"When I think, I don't have to stop."

"You mean to say you never even *asked* the name?"

"I don't *mean* to say it—I *say* it."

"You been going up to the parsonage every day to treat the woman," Bishop said, "but somehow or other you just never got around to ask who she was."

"That's right, Eli."

"Wouldn't you say that's kind of odd, Doc?"

"No, I wouldn't."

"*I* would. I'd say it's odd as a pewter dollar in a mud-hole."

"That's real odd, Eli."

"It's odder than odd, Doc—it's against nature."

"I know something that's even more against nature."

"You do? I'd like to hear it."

"Kicking that same woman out in the rain!"

"Who kicked who out in the rain?" Bishop said.

"God *damn* it, Eli!" Slocum said.

"*I* don't own Polk's store."

"Don't ever think *I* kicked her out," Polk said.

"No?" Slocum said. "Give me a good reason."

"She walked out on her own power."

"And knocked you down when you begged her to stay, I suppose. You took her by the hand, maybe, and you said, 'Miss, it's pouring down through the middle out there, and you're soaking wet. Now, why don't you sit by the stove and dry off while I fix you a cup of hot tea?' She wouldn't hear of it, though, would she? She pushed your generosity back into your face. She cussed your beard to a curl, spit in your flour-barrel, and sailed out. . . . Why, you pismire!"

"Don't ever think I'm a pismire, Doc."

"A pismire—that's what you are! And I'm going to take my trade away from you for a year!"

"You'll be back quicker. The nearest store's in Lake George."

62

"I wouldn't care if it was in Montreal. I don't trade with pismires."

"Boys," Bishop said, "so long as that nigger ain't got a name of her own, I think we ought to run one up for her."

"Me," French said, "I ain't up on nigger-names."

"I heard one called Sambo once," Piper said.

"That's a nigger-*man*," Bishop said.

"If she wasn't a woman," Polhemus said, "we could call her Lincoln."

"Lincoln!" Polk said. "Who ever heard of a nigger name of Lincoln?"

"Who ever heard of the Civil War?" Slocum said. "That's what *I* want to know."

"A nigger name of Lincoln!" Polk said. "I tell you, I'm so mad that if one come along right now, I'd hit him hard enough to straighten a cock-eye!"

"Listen," Polhemus said, "there's more nigger-Lincolns than white."

"That's what I call a crime, and don't ever think I don't."

"How's this for a nigger-woman name?" Estes said. "Ophelia."

"Ain't there a joke about Ophelia?" Harned said.

"A damn good one," Smead said. "Ophelia Oats."

"I thunk one up," Polk said. "Africa."

"You're getting warm," Bishop said.

"Australia," Confrey said.

"Lickrish," Polhemus said.

"Alabama," Hustis said.

63

"You're hot," Bishop said. "Keep a-throwing."

"Dixie," Estes said.

"Atlanta," Smead said. "Like in Georgia."

"Ah, the hell with geography," Polk said.

"The hell with *you*!" Bishop said. "This is a christening!"

Inside the Post Office, a phone-bell rang: four longs, and then a pause—and in the pause, no one spoke. Two shorts followed, and Harned went to the door.

"America . . . ," Slocum said.

Harned stopped with his hand on the knob. Above his head, in the risen warmth, the flies slowly skated figure-eights.

"America . . . ," Slocum said. "America Smith."

From behind the building, from far downhill, came the running-engine sound of the pouring Schroon. Harned drowned it in the new-shoe creak of the door.

"Thought you didn't know her name, Doc," Bishop said.

Slocum looked at him for a moment and suddenly began to laugh.

"What's so funny?" Bishop said.

Harned returned and sat down, saying, "You can go home and whale hell out of your wives, boys."

"No mail?" French said.

"Train's late. Loose rail down to Fort Edward."

"Confound that Delaware & Hudson," Slocum said.

"Expecting a letter, Doc?" Bishop said.

"Business or pleasure?" Confrey said.

"He's a little old for pleasure," Bishop said.

"Fifty-eight ain't old," Piper said.

"Fifty-eight and then some."

"If he's a good doer," Piper said, "he ain't old."

"Is she fat, Doc?" Polhemus said. "I like them fleshed up."

"I bet she's slab-sided as a cedar shake," French said.

"Come on, Doc," Bishop said. "Who's the spraddle-leg?"

"A little tear-sheet named the State of New York," Slocum said.

Bishop struck a balance on the hind legs of his chair. "I never knew she was on the town," he said.

"I sent a test-tube of blood down to the Board of Health a few days ago. I've been waiting for a report."

"Whose blood, Doc?" Bishop said, rocking the chair back to the wall. "The nigger-woman's?"

"No," Slocum said, and again he listened to the muffled plunge of distant water. "No, it belongs to one of *us* puritans."

"What's a pismire, Doc?" Polk said.

"A certain kind of ant."

"*What* kind?"

"A piss-ant, Leland."

✿

## THE PEOPLE FROM HEAVEN

### 1607 A.D.

*. . . Bid Pokahontas bring two little Baskets,*
*and I wil give her beads to make her a chaine.*

A gift? Not the longest Indian summer's day!
You gave steel for nothing, but that was all;
for all the rest we paid through the nose.
You gave something little for something large,
and if you ever got the dirty end of the stick,
it was because you were looking the other way.
You gave sweat-shop cotton for pounded corn;
you offered us words and bargained for women;
your beads came cheap: the price was Virginia!

*. . . Bid Pokahontas bring two little Baskets,*
*and I wil give her beads to make her a chaine.*

You got off to a flying start, coming by sea
and coming from the east—as in the promise—

66

and the promise being redeemed in the main,
we didn't haggle over such particulars as
the wizard-skiff, the ship of serpent-skins,
or the long white robes you said you'd wear:
your ship was wooden and your shirt iron,
but what of it? Maybe the styles had changed.

. . . *Bid Pokahontas bring two little Baskets,*
*and I wil give her beads to make her a chaine.*

We greeted you with gifts when you came ashore
(not the Indian kind—*your* kind: permanent),
but seeing our weapons (didn't you have guns?),
you got jumpy and drew blood in your first hour
on the Chesapeake, and taking our drowsy dream,
we put it back to bed till the next time,
till the next boat-load came from the east,
but meanwhile, what about the Indian brains
that mingled with the Indian corn on the beach?
What about the scalps hanging from your belts?
God damn you! What about evening the score?
(. . . To remove an arrow, break the tail clean
and pull the shaft straight through the wound.
Don't scream if it hurts. Don't be a dog. . . .)

. . . *Bid Pokahontas bring two little Baskets,*
*and I wil give her beads to make her a chaine.*

And when brought, what were the little baskets
to contain? Were they to be filled with peas,
or was it fish you wanted, or jerked flesh,
or was it maracocks, the fruit like the lemon,

67

or boiled bread, known to you as corn ponak?
What food did you need? You forgot to say. . . .
It *was* food, though, wasn't it, you farmers
that drank out of kegs and ate from the cellar;
it was food you wanted, wasn't it, you settlers
that settled on your ass? It was food, *food* . . . !

CAPT. SMITH: . . . *God (being angrie with us)*
*plagued us with such famin and sicknes*
*that living were scarce able to bury dead.*
*Onely of Sturgion did wee have great store,*
*whereon our men would so greedily surfet*
*as to bring on flux and cost many their lives;*
*the Sack, Aquavitie, and other preservatives*
*being kept onely in Capt. Wingfield's hands*
*for his owne diet and his few associates. . . .*
*Shortly after, God pleased (in our extremity)*
*to move the Indians to bring us some Corne,*
*when we rather expected they would destroy us.*

CAPT. WINGFIELD: . . . *Capt. Smith is a liar.*
*It is a lie that I did much banquit and ryot*
*before the many hungry eies of the Collony,*
*and that I served Ratcliffe with foule Corne*
*and denyed his sonne a spoonefull of beere.*
*I never did have but one squirell roasted,*
*whereof I gave part to Ratcliffe, then sick,*
*and I did never once heate me a flesh pott*
*but when the comon pott was used likewise,*
*yet often, night and daye, have other spitts*
*bene endaungered to break their backs,*

*so laden with swanns, ducks, geese, etc.!*
*I did alwaies give evry man his allowance*
*of oil, vinegar, and Canary, also Aquavitie,*
*and onely when the quantity was much reduced*
*did I seal up the rest against emergencie,*
*yet, Lord, how they did long for to supp up*
*that little remnant left in the comon store,*
*for they had emptied all their owne bottles*
*and all other that they could smell out!*

CAPT. SMITH: *. . . He has stuffed his relacyons*
*with many falsities and malycyous detractyons.*

CAPT. WINGFIELD: *. . . Twice a liar is Smith,*
*for it has been proved before his face*
*that when in Ireland he begged like a rogue*
*(without a lycence), and to such as he is,*
*I would not my name should be a companyon.*

And when the cellar and the kegs were empty,
great Oke of the Indians, how they starved,
how loudly they starved in the wilderness!
They began to die on the sixth day of August,

> *That was a good year, and the summer sun,*
> *like a kiss, sucked all day long at the corn.*

and they kept on dying for a month, or more,

> *The ears drooled wax now, green and brown.*

and as they'd lived (with noise), they died:
John Asbie went first, with bleeding bowels,
but George Flowre, taken off by the Swelling,

69

was right on his heels and forcing the pace,
and then came a Gent., one William Bruster,
found out by an arrow, and found for keeps,
and then Jeremy Alicock turned up his toes,
the toes of a Gent., slender, like fingers,
and under the daisies that same summer's day
was a certain Midwinter, an off-season Gent.,

*The corn was a forest now for red babies,*
*and on their bellies in the gloom, and silent,*
*they stalked their prey—the deadly rabbit.*

and now two more, dead as door-nails, went
arm-in-arm, and then death bagged another Gent.,
one Thomas Gore, or Gower, or some such name,
but if you think death was out of ammunition,
ask John Martine (forgive us: Martine, *Gent.*)
or dig up the upstart, dig up Rob Pennington,
a non-Gent. who stopped one in fancy company,

*And we went along the rows, counting food,*
*measuring our hope of lasting out the year,*
*and we found enough, but not an ear to spare*
*for guests come with guns in hand, demanding.*

and then Pickhouse (some said Piggase) died,
and then a big name, quite a piece of cheese,
judging from the many volleys of small shot
they fired over his grave: Bartholomew Gosnold,

*That night each of us had his say and said it,*
*and in all but one, pity ran second to hunger.*
*He made his argument with a rising inflection:*

70

*if the shoe were on the other (the Indian) foot,*
*and not strangers but Indians hungered . . . ?*

and the salute was bouncing off the Blue Ridge
when two nobodies went to unsaluted graves
(they got yesterday's lament, the Gosnold echo,
powder being for dead Gents. and live Indians),
and then, in single file, William Rods, laborer
(Rods, Roods, Rodes—spell it any way you like
as long as it's clear that he wasn't a Gent.),
and Cape Merchant Stoodie, and Throgmortine,
and Sergeant Jacob, and Mister Benjamin Beast. . . .

CAPT. SMITH: . . . *God pleased (in our extremity)*
*to move the Indians to bring us some Corne,*
*when we rather expected they would destroy us.*

POKAHONTAS: . . . Why did we *not* destroy them?
Why, being savages *inconstant in everie thing*
*but what feare constraineth them to keepe,*
*being quick to anger, craftie, and quick to run,*
*and being so enamoured of all Ornamentations*
*that they sporte dead Rats tied by the tail*
*and even greene and yellow coloured snakes,*
*which crawl and lapp and often kiss their lips,*
and why, being savages *continually in warres*
*and eateing their enemies when they kill them,*
*or any stranger if they make him their prisoner,*
why, being savages *that lick up man's spittle*
*in a barbarous fashion, like foule Dogges,*

71

*whensoever a settler spits in their mouthes,*
why, being savages *that poyson their Arrowheads
and worship Oke, the Sunne, and other Devills,
acknowledging neither a God nor a Resurrection,*
why, my people, why did we not destroy them?

✦

# STARTING FROM POLK'S

". . . I'm going home," Bishop said.

"Night," Polk said.

"Night," Bishop said.

Others too said good-night, and Bishop left the store.

"King me," Polhemus said to Pirie, and Pirie clacked down a captured checker on one that had run his blockade. "He's going home, all right—but not in a beeline."

Pirie studied the board for a sacrifice, a one-for-two. He leaned closer, stroking his nose, with thumb and fore-finger slowly stroking it. "How the hell else would he go?" he said.

"Your move," Polhemus said.

Bishop was a long time covering the mile between Polk's store and his farm on the Chestertown pike. Halfway, when he was beyond the range of the last road-lamp in Warrensburg, he swung west in a wide loop that took him across the fields to the bank of the Schroon. There, chained to a willow, a flat-bottomed rowboat rode the current, and hidden in some nearby weeds were a pair of oars. Rising from the opposite bank, a dark loom against the ground-glass glitter of the sky, was the sitting hill that held Number Four Pond. The river rapped its knuckles on the bottom of the boat. . . .

Light came from one window of the parsonage, but before the black background of trees, more did it seem as if light were entering it, a split, an idle axe of light sunk into the block of the house. The window was partly open, and moths, taking a wind-up first, pitched themselves at the glass above or the screen below, and, with a crack or a drone, bounced away. At a table in the lighted room sat Daniel Hunter and the woman.

". . . Why won't you tell me your name?" Hunter said.

"What difference would it make?" the woman said.

"It's the natural thing. Call a person by name, and you almost touch him with your hand. I like people to touch me with their hands. I like it when a man says 'Dan this' and 'Dan that,' even if nobody else is around that he can be talking to: it means there's a good feeling between him and me."

"What kind of a feeling is there when somebody says, 'Daisy, scrub the floor,' or 'Joe, shine my shoes,' or 'Mamie, I got a white man downstairs wants a change of luck.'?"

Hunter finished a pencil-curl that he had been drawing on the margin of a newspaper. "You know what they're calling you down in Warrensburg?" he said.

74

"The same as they do everywhere else: nigger."

"Not everywhere."

"Everywhere *I've* ever been."

"Not here in this house."

"Not yet," the woman said.

"Not ever."

"Why don't *you* call me a nigger?"

"I've never used the word in my life."

"I don't believe you."

"It's the truth, though."

"Why should I think you're any different? Because God calls you Dan?"

"He doesn't."

"He must have a bad feeling for you."

"Worse than good, but better than bad," Hunter said, and then he smiled. "He calls me Danny."

"What do *you* call *Him?*" the woman said. "Mister?"

"I don't call Him anything."

"Call Him Mister. He'd like it. Mister God."

"He'd think I wanted something for nothing."

"Mister God—like Mister Polk!"

"Do *you* call Him Mister?"

"I don't talk to myself."

"He'd hear you no matter how you talked—but you've got to talk."

"I've got to beg, you mean."

"Is praying begging?" Hunter said.

"It's not even as good. I've seen beggars get a handout."

75

"But never a prayer answered?"

"My people were praying before yours ever showed them how, but God's deaf. He's blind too, or He wouldn't need me to tell Him we're sick of eating dirt. And He's got no hands, or He'd touch me like He touches you. But worse than all that, when you see pictures of Him, you realize He's white! No wonder He can't hear the black race. He can smell it, but He can't hear it!"

"Sometimes He can't hear the white, either."

"What's the good of Him, then? He's busted. Your Indians would beat Him, and if He still didn't work, they'd throw Him away. Not the white man, though: he's like a cow; he never spits anything out."

"Have you spit God out?"

"I never had Him in my mouth: I was born fifty years after Lincoln was shot."

"There'll be other Lincolns."

"There'll be other shots. Why don't the *Lincolns* ever shoot?"

"They do shoot—only not with guns."

"They shoot off their mouths."

"A mouth is a dangerous weapon. A man oughtn't to be allowed to carry one without a license."

"The kind you preachers carry couldn't kill a flea in seventeen thousand years. I don't want to wait that long for a seat in a trolley-car."

"I don't blame you," Hunter said, and once more he was drawing abstractions—circles, arrows, boxes, endless spirals—on the margin of the newspaper. "I wouldn't wait that long for a seat in Heaven." The pencil executed its lead formations as if independent of the hand that held it, and he watched the automatic scribble until it began to involve his eyes. He looked up, saying, "I'm in the wrong business. People come to me for shoes and settle for soap. They want a meal, and I'm running a beauty-parlor!"

"Pray for shoes, Mister Preacher," the woman said. "Get down on your knees and pray for shoes. God'll send you a pair—right in your face!"

She picked up the pencil now, and for her too it wandered—not in multiplying patterns, but one long tangle like a heap of string. . . .

### AMERICA SMITH'S STORY

I was born twenty-eight years ago in Memphis, not in a hospital, not in a home, not in a boarding-house, not in a bed, even, or an open field: I was born on a bale of hay in a circus-tent, and I cost my father one dollar to live, the price of the hay they had to throw away because my mother bled on it, slowly at first and then suddenly to death. I cost my father a wife and a dollar, and they wanted the money then and there, they wanted the money, they said, they wanted to be paid for the spoiled hay right over the counter—not at the end of the week, not tomorrow, but *now*, you black bastard, *now*!

My father said, "Please, suh."

He said, "Please, Mister."

He said, "Please . . . ," and he could only whisper it, ". . . please, Master!"

They said, "Listen, you nigger son-of-a-bitch!"

They said, "Cough up eight bits, or we'll heave this stiff out in the road!"

They said, "You got an hour—but remember, an hour!"

My father made the dollar at the one concession along the midway where a black man could always get a job. He made the dollar letting people throw base-balls at his head, collecting one dime for every dozen rockets that bounced off his skull. It would've been easy to duck—at thirty feet, hardly anybody could've hit you twice if he tried all day—but there was no money in ducking. You were paid only for being hit. You had to get hit if you wanted to eat; you had to learn how to take a grazer down the side of your head and not be hurt any more than when you put your hat on; but knowing nothing about the tricks of dodging and slapping the canvas and making believe he was groggy, knowing only that he had to get hit one hundred and twenty times in sixty minutes, my father just put his head through that hole and let them pitch away.

It took the midway grape-vine five minutes to pass the word about the nigger with the cannon-ball for a head, and the concession did its best hour's business of the year. "EVERYBODY RIDES THE DIPSY-DOODLE! THE BOYS BRING THE GIRLS, AND THE GIRLS BRING THE BOYS! FUN, FUN, FUN FOR EVERYONE! EVERYBODY RIDES, FOLKS, EVERYBODY RIDES THE DIPSY-DOODLE!"

Everybody rode. When my father drew his pay, his head looked as if it'd been used to swab a butcher's block, and if the scars lasted the rest of his life, the dollar lasted only till he got back to the tent. The Misters and the Masters were waiting, and I was waiting, and my mother's body was waiting: there had to be money for a funeral and money for food; there had to be money for the living and money for the dead. The next day my father went into hock for a grave and a case of canned milk, and that night, with his head still bleeding, he turned up at the concession ("EVERYBODY RIDES THE DIPSY-DOODLE!") and asked for work.

He got it, and he kept it for fifteen years. For fifteen years, he earned a living avoiding death loaded, aimed, and fired at the rate of six shots for a nickel. For fifteen years, any man, woman, or child who could show a five-cent piece (but not a hunting-license) had the right to stand up to a counter and pitch six baseballs at my father's head. For fifteen years, he grinned out at a parade of white faces, looking always for one that would say with its eyes:

"Don't be ascared of me, nigger."

"I ain't going to hurt you."

"I'm only giving my kids a good time."

"I ain't such a bad guy."

"I'll chuck it easy, see?"

"I'll just lob it over."

"It's all in fun."

"I like niggers."

"They're human beings, ain't they?"

79

"Don't be ascared, nigger. Don't be so ascared."

For fifteen years, my father looked for the white face that would turn not to him, but to the owner of the concession, and say, "Duck, you white son-of-a-bitch! I'm throwing at *you*!" But the Lincolns never shoot, they only get shot at, and my father died still looking for that white face. A miner in Wilkes-Barre caught him after his sight had gone bad, and hitting him square on the top of his head, the ball dug a dent that it actually stuck in for a second. By the time it fell to the ground, my father was hanging by his chin from the canvas collar, and he was dead.

I too looked always for the white face that would say, even only with its eyes, "My hand is not raised against you." I looked for it because I knew that when I saw it, it would be time for me to speak. I have not yet spoken because I have not yet seen the face. . . .

✿

"*My* face," Hunter said. "Look at *my* face!"

Slowly the woman raised her head.

✿

## DUTCH TREAT

### 1619 A.D.

*. . . There came, about the last day of August,*
*a Dutch man o' war that sold us twenty Negars.*

You're in Virginia now, you nigger-servants,
and what's past is past—do you understand?
(Do you hear me, damn you? Do you understand?)
You'll look simple about those deaths at sea,
and if you blink, say it was sun in your eyes,
and your grub was good, and there was plenty,
and it's the lie of all lies you've ever heard
that we picked a different woman every night
and lined up stewed for a crack at her wagon—
we're Dutchmen, you understand, Dutch gents,
and before we jump a lady we ask permission;
you won't talk about the welts on your back,
you're stumped by those galls and open sores
(change of climate, maybe, or too much salt),

and the man that squawks that we had the pox,
he goes to starboard, and his fries go to port;
and, finally, nobody asked you to come along:
we was trading, see, minding our own business,
and the first thing we knew you'd stowed away;
we was on the beach, see, setting by a fire,
and some of us was running off at the mouth
*about Virginia* . . .
Mulberry, walnut, ash, elm, oak, and cypress:
enough for a new mast in every ship afloat,
enough for a new Amsterdam and one for Sunday,
enough for a new outhouse in every backyard,
enough for new shoes on every pair of feet,
and where feet are missing, for wooden legs,
enough for crutches for a race of cripples,
handles for hatchets, and cradles for guns,
beds for every man that sleeps on the ground,
tables to sit at, and a chair for every rump,
pipes and flag-poles, horse-collars and canes,
wood enough for wooden whistles, wood to burn,
more wood, man, than you can shake a stick at!
. . . *In Virginia*
they've got a fruit they call the putchamin,
green at first, then yellow, and finally red,
and when red, ripe, ripe as a woman's nipple
(I've tasted both, and it's as true as God),
and if you like cherries, you lie on your back
while the wind feeds you ox-hearts from the trees,
and for wine there's a grape named Messaminne,

or, better than the Malaga, the scuppernong,
and April strawberries, and the raspise fruit,
a little nothing that sweetens up the gullet
like a deep whiff from a snootful of flowers,
and purslin, and sorrel, and pellitory of Spain,
and the tuckahoe root, and the musquaspenne,
and sasafrage, and chinquapin, and tobacco

*. . . In Virginia*

they've got a critter they call an Aroughcun,
a tree-climbing beggar, a second-story beast
(pronounced raccoon), but sweet when roasted,
and they have another that sticks to the ribs,
the Assapanick, a squirrel flying like a bird,
and the Opassom (cat, rat, and swine in one)
that plays dead while they club it to death,
and the water Mussascus, poison on the plate,
but money in the jug, an ounce for an ounce,
because its smell is stronger than the smell
of any lady that wears it, and the Beares,
it is said, are similar to those of Muscovia,
and there are Deare too, and Hares and Conies,
and Otters, Martins, Powlecats, and Weessels,
and Minkes as well, and the silver-sided Fox,
and here only lives the Beaver, the water-dog,
but stump-legged, a sort of navigating udder
with a tail for a rudder as bare as a racket:
all these, also the Vetchunquoye, all these

*. . . In Virginia*

they've got a Blackbird with red epaulettes,

83

and the fisherman Osperaye, a flying harpoon,
and the Lanaret, harrying like a bounding ball,
stooping, striking, muffing, trying it again
through the ruffled dust, and the Goshawke,
an iron hook on iron wings that has your kill
before the smoke from your gun clears away,
and the Falcon, the projectile that returns
to sit your arm for another round of killing,
and the Eagle, the greatest devourer of all
(What did you say? Are there birds to *eat*?),
and the woods are bloody with Wilde Turkies
that spot the grass like a windfall of apples,
and always, when you walk, the earth takes wing
with the Partridge that you start up underfoot,
and the Geese come over like squalls of rain,
and if a square mile of the Chesapeake's gone,
seek it under a square Mallard mile, rippling,
and where water is, the baldhead Wigeon too,
and the Brant, and the Crayne, and a Heron
that some call the Shitepoke, and *in* the water

        . . . *In Virginia*

they've got a fish like St. George's dragon,
and another, the Todefish, that feeds on air
till a pin would bust it like a toy balloon,
and Stingrays, a pan-handled fish, and Eeles,
and white Salmonds, and three kinds of Pearch,
and Plaice, and Soles, and one with whiskers,
and the Coney-fish, and the spectrum Trowt—

wipe off your chins: no mouth has to water
in Virginia. . . .
I meant to say, no *white* mouth. Understand?
If you've got that straight, you can go ashore.

*. . . There came, about the last day of August,
a Dutch man o' war that sold us twenty Negars.*

✿

# AT THE POST OFFICE

". . . Look who's coming, boys," Bishop said.

Heads turned like electric-fans, and then all but one turned back and stopped on Bishop. Through shuttles of sunlight in the shaded road, Daniel Hunter and the woman were approaching the Post Office.

"America Smith," Polhemus said.

"A hell of a name for a nigger-woman," Polk said, "and don't ever think it ain't."

Still looking up the road, Slocum said, "A little louder, Leland."

"America Smith's a hell of a name for a nigger!"

"Louder. They mightn't have heard you."

"What if they *do* hear me, Doc?"

"Daniel might get mad."

"I ain't talking about Daniel."

"He could think you were."

A broom of wind swept dust up the road, and again the heads pivoted, this time to focus on a billowing groove in the woman's skirt. The wind idled, and the groove disappeared.

"Morning, Dan," Slocum said. "Morning, miss."

"Morning, Doc," Hunter said. "Morning, everybody."

With the point of a pen-knife, Polk nagged at a splinter in the palm of his hand; Polhemus watched the air comb smoke from the bowl of his pipe; Bishop, sitting hump-backed the wrong way of a chair, rubbed his chin on the back of it. Slocum looked from one to another, and they said nothing, and silent too were Estes, Harned, French, and Confrey.

"Missed you last Sunday, Emerson," Hunter said.

"Went fishing," Polhemus said.

"Fishing? Where?"

"Up to Viele Pond."

"Bullheads?"

"Bass."

"Since when's there been any bass in Viele Pond?"

"Put some fingerlings in last fall."

"You bring back anything?"

"A bucketful."

"Good eating, bass is," Estes said.

"Fried," Confrey said.

"Fried in bacon-grease," French said.

"You fry them in bacon-grease," Bishop said, "and the sop's most as good as the meat."

"Good eating," Estes said.

"Don't ever think they ain't," Polk said.

Hunter knew that if he spoke now, his voice would be a whisper: a point behind his navel had bloomed like a fist opening into a hand, and one of the fingers of the sensation had reached his throat.

"Mail's about due, isn't it, Ash?" Slocum said.

"Any minute, now," Harned said.

"Talking about bass," Bishop said, "Viele Pond ain't in it with Shreve's Pond."

"Shreve's Pond?" Polhemus said. "Where the hell's Shreve's Pond?"

"Up Newcomb way."

"Too far for what you get."

"I've caught me a mess of meat setting in a rocking-chair on Shreve's dam."

"Me," Polhemus said, "I don't fish from any rocking-chair."

"Funny kind of people, the Shreves," Bishop said. "I worked for them one summer."

"Ain't nothing funny about work."

"And don't ever think there is," Polk said.

"Easiest job I ever had. They used a religion that didn't let nobody lift a finger on Saturday, and me holding with the Sunday kind, I come off with two solid days of fishing every week."

"Out of a rocking-chair," Polhemus said.

"Out of a rocking-chair," Bishop said. "That is, when I could get it away from the Parson."

"Parson? What Parson?"

"Parson Peabody—the one from Shreve's church."

"A Saturday Parson. It sounds foolish to me."

"Foolish as all hell," Bishop said, "and this Peabody, he was just about the porest damn man of God I ever seen. He didn't have what to eat, so Shreve use to let him come up and fish for the pot every confounded afternoon. Far's I know, that's all he ate was fish, and he put enough of it away to make me wonder when in Christ he was going to squat down and lay himself some eggs. . . . It wasn't the *eggs* that got laid, though."

A cat came out from under the porch, flirting sleep-stiff legs, and then, salaaming, it spread its toes and clawed the dirt. The men watched it sniff its way toward the woman, passing her slowly, very slowly, accosting her, trailing its tail across her ankle, offering the length and both sides of its body—mashing her. Ignored, it sat suddenly and began to lick its shirt-front.

"Mail's awful late these days," Harned said.

### BISHOP'S STORY

I come down to the dam one Saturday afternoon, and there was Peabody, only he wasn't fishing. He was standing there reading a piece of paper, and he didn't say nothing to me till I made my first cast—matter of fact, I was just getting a nibble.

"Eli," he said, "ain't you kind of a faraway cousin to Shreve?"

"*Mrs.* Shreve," I said.

"How do you stand with *him*?" he said.

"Smart," I said. "Any time I'm looking for work, I can come up here and get me enough to knock a mule bow-legged for twenty dollars a month."

"Think you could get him to do you a favor?"

89

"I don't know. I never tried."

"Think you could get him to do *me* a favor?"

"I never tried that, either."

He looked at me for a minute, and finally he handed over the paper he was holding. It was a warrant for his arrest. I opened it up and read the charge, and then I folded it up again and handed it back without a word.

He said, "Looks pretty black, don't it?"

I said, "Is the charge true?"

"No," he said, but the word come out of his mouth like it had forty-seven letters in it. "I wonder what they'd do if they found me guilty, though."

"They'd run you out of your church, for one thing," I said.

"Is that all?" he said.

"All!" I said. "If they got specially sore, they'd run you out of town. . . . But tell me something, Peabody. Why do you come to me—a stranger?"

"I told you," he said. "I got to get Shreve to help me. *I* ain't the church here. *He* is, and if he don't vouch for me, I'm deader than a smelt."

"What you need is a lawyer," I said.

That made him so passionate his hair stood up like a lot of matches. "I need *Shreve*, Eli," he said, "and you got to help me get him! There ain't another living soul I can turn to in my hour of need. Charity is what I ask, friend—only charity. You can't wash your hands of me! You can't stand by picking your teeth while I'm being crucified!"

It so happened that I wasn't picking my teeth at the

time, and also I couldn't see nobody nailing Peabody up like a chicken-hawk, but it was too hot to get up a sweat disputing, so I said, "Man, I couldn't be no more help to you than a tit on a boar."

I figured that'd get me shut of him so's I could settle down to some honest-to-God sport, but he stuck around like a fly at a butchering-bee, and it wasn't long before his gas about charity took the edge off of fishing. I stowed my can of worms in a shady place and went up to where Shreve was setting on the porch in sock feet and looking out across as nice a five hundred acres as ever laid outdoors. Peabody tagged right along, and after begging me with his eyes some more—and not getting no place—he jumped in, clothes and all.

Shreve didn't say nothing while the Parson was putting the boots to him; he didn't even stop rocking. When Peabody got done, all Shreve wanted to know was when the hearing'd be. Funny kind of a man—Paul Shreve. I seen him stomp like a fiddler when a weasel got one of his pullets, and here was the devil catching the Parson's tail, but he wasn't even wooled up about it. Funny kind of a man.

Peabody was a funny kind of a man too. He grabbed Shreve's hand and worked it up and down like he expected to see water come pouring out of his face. "I knew it!" he said. "I knew you had a true Christian heart!"

Shreve yanked his hand away, but that didn't stop Peabody any. He made a little wigwam out of his fingers and treated us to a psalm. "Deliver me from mine enemies, O my God," he said. "Defend me from them that rise up against me. Deliver me from the workers of iniquity, and save me from bloody men. For, lo, they lie in wait for my soul. The mighty are gathering against me, not for my transgression, not for my sin, O Lord. . . ."

"For God's sake, Peabody," Shreve said, "get to hell out of here before I change my mind!"

The hearing was set for nine o'clock Monday night at the County Court at Inlet, which was a good fifty miles from the farm. Around seven, Peabody turned up at Shreve's with a man name of Whipple, the deputy that'd made the arrest, and this Whipple he was tooling a old Chevrolet sedan that all she was good for was to turn over a power-saw—if you could of got the motor out before she fell clean through into the dirt. Shreve was diked up in his Sunday best, and him and me piled onto the back seat. Whipple got the old can to rolling, and when we hit the turnpike, he opened her up to her top speed—forty an hour and awful loud.

I was glad she made such a racket because it give me a chance to talk to Shreve without Peabody or the deputy hearing me. "I want to ask you something, Paul," I said. "Are you meaning to go on the bond for this Peabody?"

"I am, Eli," he said.

"I ain't trying to be nosey," I said, "but that's going to take a hatful of hard money, and you ain't got it."

"I got the farm," he said.

92

"You're going to pledge the farm to go on a bond?" I said.

"Yes, Eli," he said.

"If you put up the farm as security," I said, "and all of a sudden Peabody takes it into his head to light a shuck out of here, you'll find yourself with a bed to sleep in, but no roof to put it under."

"I'm willing to take that risk," he said.

"But why?" I said. "Why gamble on an outsider? If you was doing it for the wife or some other relative, it'd be a different story, but you ought to know Peabody ain't going to have no more respect for you than he did for his church. Once a lowlife, always a lowlife, and if it gets too hot for him around here, he'll be smart enough to go where it's cooler, and that'll be the last you'll ever hear of him, except when you ask the sheriff why you're being run off of your land."

"I'm duty-bound," Shreve said.

"Duty-bound to who?" I said. "To some shitepoke that calls himself a Parson? Let me tell you something, Paul. Nobody goes around swearing out warrants just to pass the time of day. Where there's smoke, there's fire, and b'Jesus, I can feel it way back here! They're going to hold that Parson for trial at the next session, and between now and then he's going to ride out of here like a witch on a broom."

"You're getting mad for nothing, Eli," he said. "I'm duty-bound."

"Duty, hell!" I said.

"I don't see it like you do," Shreve said. "Peabody's

been with us here for six-seven years, ever since he got out of the Seminary, and when he come over from Lockport way to take up the post, he was lank as a snake and so pore that he didn't have no place for him and his wife to live in. . . ."

"Wait a minute," I said. "Peabody's *married?*"

"I thought everybody knew that," he said. "Well, anyhow, when the congregation found out about him being so pore, we chipped in and built him that nice little house over by the church."

"Nobody never said nothing about him having a wife when I was around," I said. "Funny thing, me not knowing that."

"Oh, I don't know," Shreve said. "You being from Warrensburg, a thing or two might get past you. Like Mrs. Peabody being bed-rid for two years now. She got that way having her second baby. . . ."

"Paul," I said, "either we just run down a pole-cat, or else somebody in this car needs a bath."

When we got to the Court House, we went up to the Judge's chambers, where the hearing was going to be held, and everybody was there waiting for us—everybody but the person that made the complain about Peabody. The Judge set at one end of a long table, and alongside of him was the Prosecutor, man name of Plumley, and across the way was a steno*graph*er to write down the case. Our crowd was bunched up at the other end of the table.

Plumley stood up, asking the Court if he could start

off, and the Judge give him leave. "Is the defendant in Court?" Plumley said.

Peabody didn't look like he knew he was being talked about, so Shreve said, "He's setting right here next to me."

The Judge looked at Shreve over a stack of law-books. "Who're you?" he said.

"Name's Paul Shreve."

"You the defendant's lawyer?"

"No, I just come along with him."

"Where you from, Mister Shreve?"

"Up by Newcomb."

"And you come all the way from there just to attend this hearing?" the Judge said.

"I ain't on trial, Judge," Shreve said.

"You're a pretty spunky old bull."

"I still ain't on trial."

"I got a good mind to hold you in contempt."

"That's your privilege, Judge."

"Go on with the case, Mister Plumley," the Judge said.

"If it please the Court," Plumley said, "I'd like to open by saying this is a hearing, not a trial, and the only issue is about the State's evidence being good and sufficient. We ain't here tonight to find out if the defendant's guilty or innocent—we got our own private opinions about that. We're here to find out if the State can show enough to warrant the Court holding him for trial later on. I'm only going to call one witness. I could call a whole lot extra, but I figure she'll turn out to be more than enough."

He went over to a door and knocked on it, saying, "Miss Marjorie Brown!"

A young girl come in the room, and after her a kind of a woman-attendant carrying a infant. The Judge called the girl over to the table and made her put a hand on the Bible while he said, "You swear to tell the truth, the whole truth, and nothing but the truth, so help you God?"

"Yes," the girl said.

"Examine her, Mister Plumley," the Judge said.

"Are you the complainant in this case?" Plumley said.

"Yes," she said.

"State your full name."

"Marjorie Rachel Brown."

"Age?"

"Going on twenty."

"Where do you live?"

"Newcomb road, up above Shreve's Pond."

"How long've you lived there?"

"All my life."

"You went to school in Newcomb?"

"Yes."

"How far?"

"Fifth grade."

"Why didn't you finish out?"

"I had to help my folks."

"Do you know a man name of Matthew Peabody?"

"Yes."

"If he's in this room, point him out."

The girl turned and looked at Peabody, but only for a second.

"Do you know what he is?" Plumley said.

"He's one of the ministers from up our way."

"How and when'd you first meet him?"

"Well, my mother was sick along about four years back, and Mrs. Peabody use to come over the house to tend to her. Mister Peabody once drove around to take her home, and that's when I met him."

"You ever work for Mrs. Peabody?"

"Yes."

"How'd that come about?"

"Well, when my mother got better, Mrs. Peabody said she liked me, and would I come over the parsonage and be the hired girl. She said she'd give me a dollar a week and meals."

"You took the job?"

"Yes."

"How long'd you work at it?"

"Pretty near four years."

"Was it hard work?"

"Yes," the girl said. "It was very hard. I had to do the house every day, and the cooking too, and in between times I had to take care of the church, polishing the wood, sweeping out, washing all the windows. It was like looking after two houses."

"What were your working-hours?"

"Well, I didn't sleep in at the parsonage, so I had

to get up around five to get things going at home. Then I went to Mister Peabody's place—it was a couple of miles to walk there—and I worked from seven in the morning till after supper. Then I use to walk home."

"Mrs. Peabody ever help you out around the parsonage?"

"Oh, yes. She was nice to me and didn't make me do nothing extra special—just what had to be done. It's just there was a whole lot to do, that's all. She use to give me a hand when she had time, but that didn't last very long."

"No? Why not?"

"She got sick when she had her second baby."

"And then you had to do all the work yourself?"

"Yes."

"And naturally it took you longer?"

"Yes," the girl said. "Sometimes it was along after nine when I started out for home."

"After finishing up at the parsonage, did you ever go out at night?"

"How could I?"

"I asked you if you ever *did*, Miss Brown."

"Maybe twice a year," the girl said, "and then only to something going on around the church. The last two years, though, I didn't get out even once. I didn't see even one movie, and I didn't go to a single dance down in the town with the other young girls and fellows. I hardly ever seen them less I passed them on the road."

"You always went home alone?"

"Yes."

"Always?"

"All but once."

"And when was that?"

"About a year back."

"You remember that night?"

"Yes."

"You remember everything that happened?"

"Yes."

"Tell us about it in your own words."

"Well, I put in a full day at the house," the girl said, "and on top of that, there was a meeting at the church in the afternoon, and I had to tidy it up when I was done doing the supper dishes, so when I was leaving the parsonage to go home, I was tireder than usually. I felt so bad I just couldn't stand it no more, and there I was crying in the road when Mister Peabody drove up in the old Chevrolet sedan that every so often he use to loan off of a deputy name of Whipple. Mister Peabody asked me what was the matter, but I couldn't bring myself to tell him account of his wife was so sick, and he had enough troubles without me making a complain. He said I shouldn't cry, and everything would come out all right if I only have faith, but I kept on crying, it seems like I just couldn't stop, and finally he said he'd drive me home in the Chevrolet."

"What happened in the car, Miss Brown?"

"Well, instead of him taking me straight home, he went out the road towards Blue Mountain Lake, saying I worked so hard indoors all day that maybe what I needed was a breath of fresh air. When we got about

99

five miles out, he turned the Chevrolet off onto that back road that goes through the woods to Jennings Forge. I said what're we going in here for, and he said he wanted to stop the car and talk to me, and it wouldn't do for anybody to see him. I said why didn't he want to get seen, and he said people'd talk if they knew the Parson was out at night with such a pretty girl. That's what he said—that I was pretty—and I liked him saying I was pretty, so I forgot to ask him what the people'd talk about. When we got a few miles up the road, Mister Peabody stopped the car and turned off the lights, and then he set back and put his hand on my shoulder, saying I should tell him all of my troubles. He acted very kind, and he patted me just like he was my own father, so I told him why I was feeling so low, and all the time he was saying, 'I know, I know, my child,' and afterwards he said the Twenty-third Psalm out loud to me, and then he just set there not saying nothing for a while because he was crying, and I felt so sorry for him that I didn't push him away when he come over closer and put his arms around me. I felt sorry about him being so pore, and having all that worry with his wife, and anyhow it was just like me getting a fellow all to myself like the other girls in the town, so I didn't push him away."

"What happened in the car that night?"

"Why should I of pushed him away? He was kind to me."

"What happened in the car that night?"

"He said we should go in the back seat, there **was**

more room there, and I done like he wanted me to. Girls use to tell me that fellows got fresh when they took you out alone some place, but not Mister Peabody. He was kind, and I wouldn't make him take his hands away."

*"What happened in the car that night?"*

"Oh, what do you *think* happened?"

"I *know* what happened," Plumley said, "but I got to get your statement on record."

The girl didn't answer, but nobody was watching her, anyway. They was looking at Peabody, and all he could do was fiddle with his hands.

Shreve got up and said, "Your Honor, I think it'd be a nice thing if we just took what the girl means for granted."

The Judge swang on him, saying, "Mister, what business've you got butting in on the direct examination? Sit down and keep your two cents out!"

"I just wanted to make it a little easier on the girl," Shreve said.

"You're short five dollars, Mister," the Judge said. "Plank it down on your way out!"

"Finish your story, Miss Brown," Plumley said.

"After we done it, Mister Peabody drove me home in the Chevrolet," the girl said. "I kept on working at the parsonage, but we didn't do nothing like that again for quite a while. Then one night Mrs. Peabody was took very bad with fainting-spells, and the doctor give us some medicine she should take, saying it'd be a good idea to have a woman in the house the rest of the night. Mrs. Peabody was always good to me, so I said I'd stay if they wanted me to. I looked in on Mrs. Peabody once or twice, but she appeared like she was resting easy, and then around twelve o'clock I went in again, and that time she was fast asleep. When I come out of the bed-chamber, there was Mister Peabody standing in the hall."

"What happened in the hall, Miss Brown?"

"The same as in the Chevrolet. We done it twice."

"What happened after that?"

"After four-five months I got big, and I had to stop working at the parsonage."

"Did you have a child?"

"Yes."

"When?"

"Couple of months back."

"And how long was that after the first time you had relations with Peabody?"

"Ten months."

"Where was the child born?"

"Tupper Lake County Hospital."

"And where is it now?"

"Over there," the girl said, pointing at the kid the attendant was holding.

"One more question, Miss Brown," Plumley said. "Did you ever in your life have relations with anyone else but Peabody?"

"No, never in my life."

Plumley turned to Peabody. "If you think it'll get

you anywheres, Mister Parson, you can ask the witness some questions."

"I haven't got any questions to ask her," Peabody said.

"You don't say!" Plumley said, kind of surprised. "She give pretty strong testimony."

"That's true," Peabody said.

"And you don't want to try and break her down?"

"No," Peabody said. "I don't want to try and break her down."

Shreve spoke up. "Why don't you tell your side of the story, Mister Peabody? You've got a right to defend yourself."

Peabody went down to the other end of the table, and the Judge put him through that Bible business. "You swear to tell the truth, the whole truth, and nothing but the truth, so help you whatever kind of a God you worship?"

"I do," Peabody said.

The Judge give him about a minute to stand there dumb, and then he said, "Well . . . ?"

"Well, what?" Peabody said.

"What've you got to say for yourself?"

"I haven't got nothing to say," Peabody said. "You want to ask questions, I'll answer them."

Plumley said, "I got some questions, all right, but first I want to warn you that anything you say might be used against you. You understand that?"

"Yes," Peabody said.

"First, is it true that Miss Brown use to work for you?"

"Yes."

"Second, is it true that you once took her riding in a Chevrolet sedan?"

"Yes."

"Is it true that you went up the Jennings Forge road?"

"Yes."

"Is it true that you parked the car in the woods?"

"Yes."

"Is it true that you deliberately took advantage of the innocence of a girl that'd served you faithfully for four years, that you seduced her, Mister Parson, and put her in a family way?"

"Yes, Mister Plumley."

For a couple or three seconds, Plumley stared at Peabody like he thought he was being codded, and then when it sunk in that the Parson went and confessed, he sailed into him like he meant to tear him wheel from axle.

"Why'd you do it?" Plumley said. "How could you forget your church, your position, your wife and children? Ain't you got any charity? Ain't you got any conscience? Ain't the fear of God tromping around in your chest? Why'd you do it?"

"My wife is sick, Mister Plumley."

Plumley's voice went up high and busted. "You hypocrite! You faker! You Judas! Do you call yourself a man of God? Why, you've spit in God's face!"

"I'm guilty, Mister Plumley. *I'm guilty!* What more do you want?"

Plumley turned to the Judge. "I ask Your Honor for a ruling on the testimony."

"The defendant's held for trial," the Judge said.

"Will Your Honor set a day?"

"Two weeks from tomorrow," the Judge said. "Has the defendant got a bondsman?"

A old man in a Sunday suit stood up. "Name's Paul Shreve, Judge," he said.

I went over to Whipple and asked him to come out and have a smoke while they was fixing up about the bond, and damn if he didn't ask Peabody to come along.

☼

Across the road, on the lawn of the Adirondack Inn, a boy lay on his belly and crawled inch-by-inch through an ambush of grass. Clamped in his teeth he held a tomahawk, and smearing one of his cheeks was its red and sticky blade. And now slowly, with no leaf rustling, with no joint cracking, with no breath passing in or out, with the patient and supremely silent craft of the woodsman, the boy raised his weapon, a cherry lollipop, and split the skull of his enemy—nothing. Then, suddenly forgetting the murder, he sat up in the grass and bit off a piece of the candy.

Hunter climbed the four steps from the road to the porch, and sitting on the railing near Bishop, he put his hand on the man's shoulder.

"Why did you tell that story, Eli?" he said.

"It's a true one," Bishop said. "I call it 'Once In A Sedan And Twice Standing Up.' "

"I asked you why you told it, Eli."

"Didn't you like it, Dan?"

"No, I didn't, Eli."

"That's too bad, Dan."

"Does that mean you're sorry?"

"No, I just mean it's too bad."

"Please don't tell any more stories like that."

"Why not, Dan?"

"Because I'm not a preacher all the time."

"I didn't think you was, Dan."

"I'm a human being too, Eli."

"That's a fine thing to be, Dan."

"The finest. I eat food, I drink water, and I breathe in and breathe out—just like other human beings—and I've got a pair of arms, and a brain to move them around, and I've got a bellyful of blood, and damn it, sometimes it gets in my eyes."

"That makes you just like all the rest of us, Dan."

"I wish you'd remember that, Eli."

"And if you got the chance, Dan, you'd do just like we do, wouldn't you?"

"Yes, I would."

"Like driving a bargain, maybe?" Bishop said.

"Maybe."

"Or like taking a snort once in a while?"

"Once in a while."

"Or like using plain language if it happened to come to you?"

"The plainer, the better."

"Or even like looking twice at a woman if she struck your eye?"

"That's right, Eli—if she struck my eye."

"That's what I figured, Dan. I always knew you wasn't any angel."

"There's one thing I *wouldn't* do, though, Eli."

"What's that, Dan?"

"I wouldn't tell stories like the one I just heard."

"Ain't we back where we started?" Bishop said.

"Pretty near, Eli."

"And now you want to say what you're going to do if I don't take the hint. That right, Dan?"

"Yes, Eli."

"Well, say it, Dan. Say what you'll do if I keep right on telling my stories."

"I'll kill you, Eli."

✤

### AT THE POOR HOME

The only sound in Room 8 came from the brass guts of an alarm-clock squatting on a bedside table in a full skirt of lamplight: it was almost twelve now, and the minute-hand was coming up tick-by-tick to join the hour-hand, and soon the clock would sit with its eyes hidden, as if in shame. The walls of the small room were adorned only with calendars, and of these there were many, lurid and varied—each, however, with a pencil-ring around the numerals of the same early-summer day. In a group at the foot of the bed stood Dan Hunter, Doc Slocum, America Smith, Grace Paulhan, and Aaron Platt. The bed was Little Johnny Littlejohn's, and he was a hundred clock-clicks under a hundred years old.

The clock cleared its throat and rang—it rang, and, ringing, it tap-danced across the table-top like a ten-cent toy; it danced, and, dancing, it died, for it reached the edge of the table and fell to the floor. The hammer beat the bell feebly for a while, and then there was no sound in Room 8, not even the cheap sound of tin time. Little Johnny Littlejohn was a hundred years old.

Slocum bent over the old man, saying, "Daddy, we kept you going."

The old man snared a tear with his tongue. "That little fool dream," he said. "It come true. It come true, Doc."

"It *had* to come true, Daddy. God couldn't have been that mean."

"Daddy," Hunter said, "would you mind if I spoke a little prayer?"

"I'll speak my own prayers," the old man said, and he looked up at the ceiling. "Lord, it ain't everybody could get to be a hundred years old on the kind of pancakes they feed you at this dump, and I'm damn grateful for having a belly to do what my plates was never meant for. I only got one complain to make, Lord, and that is: *Where in the holy hell is my birthday-presents?*"

The paper on parcels rattled. America Smith had a pair of hand-made red woolen mittens, and Grace Paulhan a tasseled scarf to match. Aaron Platt had brought a pipe and a one-pound jar of Prince Albert, and Dan Hunter's gift was a black silk four-in-hand with a pattern of American flags. The old man turned to Doc Slocum.

"How about you, bub?" he said.

From a canvas case, Slocum drew an old and rusted rifle. "I found this in a junk-shop in Albany, Daddy," he said. "I thought it might remind you of Antietam."

"A Sharps carbine, b'Jucks!" the old man said. "Give it here, bub. You'll hurt yourself." He took the piece, balanced it, and finally fitted it to his shoulder and face, saying, "I wish it was loaded. I'd blow today right out of that calendar."

"And your thumb along with it," Slocum said.

But the word *calendar* had stayed with the old man, and now as he put the carbine down across his knees and picked at a scale of rust on the trigger-guard, he said, "I guess I won't have to write for no calendar this year. The Finch & Pruyn Lumber Company, the Saratoga Race Track, the Delaware & Hudson—they can send their calendars to somebody else. I ain't never going to see a hundred and one. . . ."

✿

## CAPTAIN SHRIMP, AND CERTAIN OTHERS

### 1620 A.D.

"COME . . . !" we cried, and from mouth to mouth,
from Indian on the beach to Indian in the trees,
from savage running to savage standing still,
from one foule Dogge to another foule Dogge,
the rumor that they'd come back from the east
with birds, and there was perfume in the air:
"Come! come to see the people from Heaven!" . . .
That was a hundred and twenty-eight years ago,
and now I say this—an Indian to other Indians,
a savage to savages, and a Dogge to many Dogges:
what was rumor then is rumor still and always,
because if truly these are people from Heaven,
why are they so God damned familiar with hell?

✿

# AFTER CHURCH

WHEN the services broke, the sun was almost directly overhead, and shadows clung like young to the feet of the dispersing congregation. No one spoke, and except for the clench of stepped-on gravel, the Sunday noon was silent as feet and their broods of shadow moved toward a row of cars and carriages. The last to leave the church were America Smith and Dan Hunter, and addressed by none in passing, they greeted none, but in their wake a foam of conversation rose to the surface of the quiet. Three people were waiting for them on the path that bordered the road—Doc Slocum, Grace Paulhan, and Aaron Platt.

Eli Bishop watched the group start downhill. "There goes one hell of a Sunday dinner-party," he said. "Preacher, doctor, murderer, whoor, and nigger—one of each!"

✿

## THE FIRST KNEE ON CANADA

### 1632 A.D.

WE CAUGHT fireflies in the darkening meadows,
and threading them into on-and-off festoons,
we hung them up before the altar and the Host,
and they made light for God, Ghost, and Jesus
while we, adoring, put the first knee on Canada.

*Who's that nailed to the cross, Black-robes?*
*If he's an enemy, let your chief eat his heart,*
*but if he's an Oke, you've killed yourselves*
*unless you burn tobacco and invite him down.*
*Take our advice about such things, Black-robes;*
*listen to us, for we know the ways of the land,*
*and you, on your knees like women making food,*
*have already offended us with your ignorance:*
*fireflies must not bow down to graven images!*

We said, "Unhappy infidels (meaning Dogges),
you that live in smoke only to die in flames,
repent you and choose between Heaven and hell!"

*We said, "The sky is the palace of thunder,"*
*but it was clear that they did not understand.*
*"The sky," we said, "the blue wigwam overhead,*
*the sky is the home of thunder, understand?*
*and thunder is a turkey-cock, a cock but a man,*
*yet in one thing he is neither man nor bird,*
*in one thing strange to all that walk or fly:*
*he comes forth only when the wigwam is gray.*
*He comes forth like a man, though, grumbling,*
*and he flies down to earth to gather snakes,*
*snakes and other objects that we call Okies,*
*and if you see flashes of fire as he descends,*
*that fire attends the beating of his wings,*
*and if the grumbling now and then is violent,*
*be sure his children have been brought along.*
*Indian babies know all this. Why do you stare?"*

"Which do you choose," we said, "Heaven or hell?"

*We said, "Heaven is a good place for Frenchmen."*

"Which do you choose," we said, "Heaven or hell?"

*We said, "The French will not feed us in Heaven."*

"Which do you choose," we said, "Heaven or hell?"

*We said, "Do they hunt in Heaven? do they dance?*
*do they make war or hold festivals in Heaven?*
*If not, we will not go, for idleness is evil."*

"Which do you choose," we said, "Heaven or hell?"

*We said, "If our dead are in hell, as you say,*
*if for want of a few sprinkled drops of water*
*our babies live in hell, we would go there too."*

We wrote, "We find that pictures are invaluable
in bringing about conversions among the Hurons;
we have learned that these holy representations
are half the battle to be fought against them.
We desire some more showing souls in perdition,
and if you sent a few drawn on paper or canvas,
with three, four, or even five tormenting devils
visiting different punishments on the damned,
one with pincers, another applying fire, etc.,
they would have a lasting effect on the savages,
especially if the drawings were made distinct,
if they revealed misery and rage and despair
written on the (red) faces of the condemned."

*We said, "We see plainly that your God is angry*
*because we will neither believe nor obey him.*
*Ihonatiria, where first you taught his word,*
*is ruined, and then you came here to Ossossané,*
*and here too we were skeptical of your God,*
*and now the wolves pick Ossossané's bones,*
*and then you went up and down our country,*
*and from rising to setting sun you found none*
*to do the bidding of your God and bow down,*
*and therefore the pestilence is everywhere."*

We said, "Do you believe, then? Do you repent?"

*We said, "How eager you are for a humble 'Yes,'*
*but we know a better cure, we know a medicine*
*that will work more wonders than wafer or wine:*
*we will shut you out now from all our houses*
*and stop our ears when your God gives tongue,*
*and then, neither hearing him nor seeing you,*
*we will be innocent again, as before you came,*
*and avoid the penalty of refusing to be saved."*

Our mission suffered from no lack of visitors,
for the Hurons flocked there to see the marvels
that we had wisely brought with us from France,
and in expectant silence, from dawn to evening,
they squatted on the ground before the door,
waiting for a performance of the repeating-lens,
which showed them the same object eleven times,
and the magnifying-glass, wherein a simple flea
became so monstrous as to overwhelm the eye,
and the mill, which they never tired of turning,
and lastly, the miracle of miracles, a clock
that struck the hours from one to twenty-four:
they thought it was alive and asked what it ate,
and when at the final stroke we cried "Stop!"
and it stopped, their admiration was boundless.
The incomprehensible mysteries of our Faith,
the clock, the glass, the lens, and the mill—
all this served to win the Indians' affection.

*They proposed that a number of young Frenchmen*
*should be invited to settle amongst our people*
*and wed our daughters in solemn and holy form,*

*but we said, "Of what use is so much ceremony?*
*If these young Frenchmen desire our daughters,*
*they will come and take them when they please;*
*they will do again what they have done before."*

They led Brébeuf out and bound him to a stake,
but if they hoped he would plead for his life
(for what God gave, and only God could take away),
the red wretches were doomed to disappointment,
even as they were doomed to everlasting flames.
The priest addressed the converts he had made,
promising Heaven if they retained their faith,
thus angering the Iroquois, and to silence him
they scorched him with coals from head to foot,
and when (as if they were bound and he free)
he spoke further, they cut away his lower lip,
and they thrust a red-hot iron down his throat.
His mouth made no words now, nor uttered pain,
and they tried a subtler means to overcome him,
for they took it to be an augury of disaster
if torture failed: they brought forth Lalemant,
that Brébeuf might see his agony and cry aloud
for his brother in Christ if not for himself.
Naked under his cassock of pitch-soaked bark,
Lalemant fell to his knees, saying these words
after the sainted Paul: "We are made a spectacle
unto the world, and to angels, and to men!"
whereupon the red devils put fire to the bark,
and Lalemant blazed up like a canoe on a beach,
but the only sound from Brébeuf was an "Ave."

Frenzied, they made him a collar of hatchets,
heated till they smoked like stones from hell,
and hung it around his neck to smoke out fear,
but he was grateful, as if they had healed him,
as if it were proud flesh they had burned away,
and he gave them a prayer in payment for pain.
Then they poured boiling water over his head,
saying that the Iroquois too knew how to pay,
that their hot water was for the Jesuit cold:
"Now we baptize you, Black-robe," they cried,
"that you may be happy in your white Heaven!"
and they tore strips from his limbs and body
and devoured this unholy food before his eyes,
saying, "The more a man suffers on the earth
(so you say), the happier he will be in Heaven,
and desiring to make you the happiest of all,
we torment you badly because we love you well."
But he sanctified their feast with a blessing,
and they scalped him and laid open his breast,
and they came in a crowd to drink his blood,
thinking thus to imbibe some part of his valor,
but he was dead, and his valor was in Paradise.

*We do not pretend, like the people from Heaven,*
*that each of us is a Manitou in his own right,*
*we do not pretend that we are more than men,*
*and being men, we endure the illnesses of men,*
*among which we rank the sense to know a friend.*
*You are not our friends, you people from Heaven,*
*you are not our friends, you that speak of God*

117

*and teach the Word, the Word being "Mine! Mine!"*
*You are no man's friend, you traders from Heaven*
*that offer a word and would take our world away!*

"Which do you choose," we said, "Heaven or hell?"

*"We choose Heaven, but not for us—for Brébeuf.*
*He was brave, like an Indian, and in admiration*
*we give you this gift as a shroud for his body*
*when the time comes to send him on his journey:*
*it is a coat of bear-skin that our women made,*
*and in your cold Heaven it will keep him warm."*

✿

# AT GRACE PAULHAN'S

"ANYBODY still hungry?" Grace said.

Doc Slocum opened his vest. "I'm all swole up like a toad."

"How about you, Aaron?"

"If I put any more chicken or mutton into me," Platt said, "I'd go to bed a-blattin' and wake up a-crowin'."

"Miss Smith?"

"I had enough," the woman said.

"Another cup of coffee, Dan?"

"Sure."

"Coffee isn't eating," Slocum said. "Pour me some too, Gracie."

"Company," Platt said, lighting the twist of a hand-made cigarette.

A car stopped in the driveway. Letting the motor idle, Eli Bishop climbed out, followed by Emerson Polhemus and Mark Lomax.

Grace went to the screen-door, and through the mesh, as they came upon the porch, she said, "Today is Sunday."

"Let them in," Slocum said. "Maybe they just dropped by for a good old foot-washing."

The three men entered, pausing near the door. The running motor beat imperfect time, and a wordless moment palpitated.

"Sit down," Grace said.

"We'll stand, if it's all the same," Lomax said.

"It's all the same," Grace said. "Coffee?"

"We get plenty to eat at home," Lomax said.

"And plenty of everything else?" Slocum said.

"Don't get personal, Doc."

"When three of the best citizens in town come snuzzling around a whorehouse on a Sunday afternoon, I always get personal."

"We was sent by the congregation," Polhemus said.

"To do what?"

"To see Dan Hunter."

"That's him behind the cake," Slocum said.

"Did they tell you to look for me here, Emerson?" Hunter said.

"We seen you come in."

"You mean watched, don't you?"

"What's the difference?" Polhemus said.

"A lot," Hunter said. "I don't like being spied on."

"We ain't spying, Dan."

"What do you call it, then?"

"We call it looking out for the church."

"The church is up the hill," Hunter said.

"The church is wherever the preacher is," Polhemus said.

120

"Is that a fact, Emerson?"

"If *it* ain't, *God* ain't," Polhemus said.

"And He's *all* fact," Lomax said.

"Then take your hats off," Hunter said.

"What's our hats got to do with it?" Lomax said.

"You're in church. Take your hats off."

"Mine stays put," Polhemus said.

"Take your confounded hats off, or get out!" Hunter said.

"I don't take my hat off in no whoorhouse!" Lomax said.

"You don't even take your shoes off," Slocum said.

The straggling cylinders of Bishop's car fell into step, and for a few paces the motor marched like a single pair of feet. Then once more the rhythm went to pieces.

"Carburetor?" Lomax said.

"Timer," Bishop said.

"Take your hats off, boys," Polhemus said, and as he spoke he removed his own.

"Emerson," Hunter said, "I can hear you now."

"Folks don't like the company you keep, Dan."

"Give them names."

"They don't like Gracie Paulhan, for one."

"Why not? She belongs to our congregation."

"Maybe, but she's on the town."

"She can still go to church."

"Not with me, she can't!" Polhemus said.

"You're pretty choosy for a whorehouse-keeper," Hunter said.

"I ain't any whoorhouse-keeper."

"Don't you own this piece of property, Emerson?"

"Sure, but that don't put me in the business."

"I hear different. I hear the rent changes according to the number of customers."

"That's a round and rolling lie, Dan!"

"Maybe yes, maybe no."

"If Gracie says I'm sliding the rent, she's lying!"

"If she says you're sliding the rent," Hunter said, "you're sliding it!"

"Do you take a whoor's word over mine?"

"I take *anybody's* word over yours, Emerson."

"I want some respect!" Polhemus said. "God damn it, I want some respect!"

"We ain't getting no place," Lomax said.

The motor fluttered, and the car laughed heartily and died. Bishop went out to throw the switch.

"Who else does the congregation object to?" Hunter said.

"If it's me, Emerson," Slocum said, "you can pay your bill and start doctoring with the vet."

Bishop returned to the porch and leaned against the door-jamb.

"They object to this nigger," Polhemus said.

"Do they *say* 'nigger'?" Hunter said.

"They say 'nigger.'"

"Do *you* say 'nigger'?"

"Yes, *I* say 'nigger.'"

"You can put your hat on now, Emerson."

"I ain't cold, Dan."

"No, but you're leaving."

"When I finish talking."

"I could swear you just said goodbye."

"Couldn't of. I still got the itch to beat my gums together."

"Do you still say 'nigger'?"

"No."

"What *do* you say, Emerson?"

"Negro."

"Louder, Emerson. Your gums are soft."

"Negro!"

"Now, what were you saying about Miss Smith?"

"She's got to stop living up to the parsonage."

"Why?" Hunter said.

"Matter of fact, she's got to get out of town."

"Why?"

"We don't want her around."

"Why?"

"I guess that's all we come here to say, Dan."

"Were you told to wait for an answer?"

Polhemus shook his head. "We didn't ask no questions."

✿

## LAND OF BEANS AND GOD

### 1691 A.D.

(BROTHER Narragansetts and other russet Dogges,
Pequots, Patuxents, Tarrantines, and Pokanokets,
I bring you from Salem heap big English love.
*What's love, brother? Is it something to eat?*
I bring, after being spat upon only seven times,
I bring you fish-hooks and doctored fire-water,
I bring buckles, buttons, and bolts of shoddy,
I bring a Bible and two shoes for the left foot.
*What's love, brother? Is it good with meat?*)

There shall be found out amongst us none, none
that causeth his son to pass through Fire, none
that consulteth with the familiar Spirits, none
that employeth a Wizzard or a Divination—none:
for they are Witches that practise these things,
and (Ex.22.18) we shall not suffer them to live!

We accuse you of irregular Strength in Lifting
and such other and prodigious Pranks and Feats

as only a Diabolical Assistance would explain:

*I seen him grab a gun with a six-foot bar'l*
*(I couldn't of budged it with block and fall)*
*and hold it at arm's-end like it was a pistol,*
*and once he took that self-same fowling-piece*
*(it weighed ten stone if it weighed ten ounces),*
*and just by sticking his thumb in the muzzle,*
*he twirled it overhead like I'd do with a hat.*
*I ast him where a puny man got such strenkth,*
*and he said, "Brother, a Indian's helping me,"*
*but the only one in sight looked kind of limp*
*because he was hanging by the neck from a tree.*

We accuse you of preternatural use of the Eye,
and urging the signature of names upon a Book,
and, failing, of visitations in sundry Shapes
and being Cat, Cock, or Rodent, as you please:

*He went by one day with a book under his arm,*
*and straight off my little boy fell in a fit*
*that pretty near scared my front teeth out.*
*I worked over him till I was blue in the face,*
*but the bluer I got, all the blacker the fit,*
*and finally a neighbor had to give an advice:*
*"Hang the boy's blanket in the chimney-corner,*
*and, come morning, if there's anything in it,*
*chuck it in the fire and burn hell out of it."*
*You know what I found in that blanket next day?*
*A toad, b'Christ, and bigger than your head!*
*He stunk up the parlor like Old Horny himself,*
*but I laid ahold of him with a pair of tongs*

125

*and give him some of his own in the fire-place,*
*and no sooner did he get a taste of them coals*
*than he made a flash like a pan of gunpowder,*
*and he went up in smoke and clean disappeared.*

We accuse you of torments with Invisible Hands,
of biting, pinching, and vexatious Prickings,
of producing Phlegm, Fever, and Running sores,
Blindness, Tumors, fits, and the Bloody Flux:

*She didn't never have a sick day in her life*
*up to the time he first laid his eyes on her,*
*and now, b'God, she don't ever have a well one!*
*She's gimpy on the on-side and then on the off,*
*and as often as not she's plumb stiff all over,*
*and if she ain't on fire, she's froze up solid,*
*and when she ain't deef, she's dumb and daft.*
*I'm talking about my daughter—not my horse—*
*but she's got the heaves, and she breaks wind*
*so's two men can't hold a carpet to a keyhole,*
*and all day long she hawks up clams of phlegm*
*with nails and crooked pins and other hardware,*
*and when she tries to say 'Heaven' or 'Christ,'*
*her tongue crawls down its hole like a snake,*
*but you give her 'Hell' to chaw on, or 'Devil,'*
*and, b'Jesus, she'll talk a blue streak, saying,*
*"That bites, but it makes me speak right well!"*

We accuse you of making a League with the Devil,
giving you the power of Levitation and Estoppel:

*I'm a-driving my cart past his house one day*
*(which if he built it any closer to the road,*

126

he'd be living acrost the way from himself),
and my hub lays a scratch alongside his wall.
I gum up my wheel lots more than his paint-job,
but he sasses me a good fifteen to the dozen
and swings threats around his head like a cat.
Now, him being a kind of spleeny little sprat,
I don't let all that gas of his bother me any:
I give him a regret and go about my business,
but when I try going through some gate-posts,
just like I done with that rig for ten years,
damn if I don't get stuck betwixt and between
even though nothing's holding me back but air,
and damn if I don't have to go fell them posts
before I can stir a inch one way or the other!

We accuse you of Mischief on the heels of Cursing:
Him and me, we once got into a little dispute
(I disremember what about: the weather, maybe),
but if it rared up fast, it fizzed out faster,
and it was done before it begun—or was it?
I say "Was it?" on account of two good reasons.
One: I took the nosebleed after that argument,
and there wouldn't nothing stop it but prayer.
And two: me that never had a louse in my life,
all of a sudden I come up lousier than a monkey;
I was crawling even when I was standing still;
I was et up setting, and I was et up on the hoof;
I tried soap, psalms, and other kinds of poison,
but finally I had to build me a nice bonfire
and get rid of every stitch outside of my pelt.

127

We accuse you of entering upon women Entranced:

   a) *He come one night when I was laying in bed,*
   *and after throwing a spell into the old man,*
   *he set down on top of me for two solid hours.*
   b) *He pulled pretty near the same stunt on me,*
   *and if he didn't stick out the full two hours,*
   *at least he done a sight more than just squat.*
   c) *For a wee man, he was quite a night-walker:*
   *he come to me one time in the shape of a rabbit,*
   *but he could of give a rabbit cards and spades.*
   d) *You ask me, he could spare the Big Casino:*
   *he swore he'd rip out my privities and bowels*
   *if I so much as made a move or opened my face,*
   *but I fooled him—I didn't put up any fight.*
   e) *I wake up all at once in the dead of night,*
   *and there he is, poking about the bed-clothes;*
   *I'm scared pink, but anyhow I let out a holler,*
   *saying, "The whole armor of God be between us!"*
   *and phutt! he's gone like a busted soap-bubble!*
   *I'm scared so loose now I got to go make water,*
   *and there I am, bare-back on the chamber-pot,*
   *when something picks me up (pot, water, and all)*
   *and shakes me out like a apron full of crumbs!*
   *Come daylight, I tell myself it's only a dream,*
   *but there's one fact teases me and always will:*
   *every time I use that pot it throws off sparks.*

We accuse you of attending Hellish Randezvouzes
and practising Magic with the Powers of the air:

   *He hires me once to wreck a old cellar-wall*
   *(it holds up the kitchen, but it's his house,*

*and so long as the place don't cave in on me,*
*I'm glad to get the work and take the wages),*
*so I'm slamming away with my sledge down there,*
*and finally I hit a stone that don't ring true.*
*A couple of good shots, and she comes unstuck,*
*and out pours the damnedest assortment of junk*
*that ever a man put together this side of hell:*
*poppets made of hair, hog's bristle, and rags;*
*pins without a head, and heads without a pin;*
*a sackful of toe-nails, and a black cat's ear;*
*a broken broom, a dead mouse, and a fake nose;*
*a witch-cake of pebbles, corn-meal, and blood;*
*a punkin, and a hymn-book printed upside-down.*
*I ask him, "What for you saving all this crap?"*
*and he says, cool as a witch's tit, "What crap?"*
*and I'm stumped—because the crap ain't there!*

We accuse you of having the Markings of a Witch
(Hidden Teats, sunken Flesh, and Webbed Feet),
and using them to reverse the course of Nature:
*It was raining pitchforks with the tines down,*
*and it was no good walking unless you had fins,*
*but that didn't stop him coming in dry as a bone*
*and slapping dust off himself fit to choke you.*
*I said (and there was others there to hear me),*
*I said, "Man, I couldn't keep that rain off me*
*except I grew more feathers than a duck's behind,"*
*and all he said was, "I scorn to be drabbled!"*

We accuse you of Rebellion against the Church:
a) *He said death is sure, but tithes are surer.*
b) *He said he believed in gynecandrical dancing.*

c) *He said he favored gimp, ribbon, and galloon.*
d) *He said if some went hungry, all were damned.*
e) *He said Indians go to Heaven, and Negars too.*
f) *He said there was no hell but here in Salem.*
g) *He said all he knew about Christ was hearsay.*
h) *He said if he was Satan, he'd want to be God.*
i) *He said if he was God, he'd want to be a man.*
j) *He said he was a man, so he'd smoke on Sunday.*

There shall be found out amongst us none, none
that causeth his son to pass through Fire, none
that consulteth with the familiar Spirits, none
that employeth a Wizzard or a Divination—none:
for they are Rebels that practise these things,
and behold, Rebellion is as the sin of Witchcraft!
If you would answer this, brother, answer now. . . .

(Brother Narragansetts and other russet Dogges,
he said, "The brother shall deliver up the brother,"
Pequots, Patuxents, Tarrantines, and Pokanokets,
he said, "Beware of men, for they will scourge you,"
and, angered, they tied a rope around his neck
and stood him on a branch in the two-legged tree,
and once more, then, they nagged him for speech,
but he had spoken, and he was done with words,
so they cut the branch, and the world fell away,
and soon, spinning slowly in the wind, he died.
*What's love, brother? Tell us more about love!*)

✿

# AROUND WARRENSBURG

### LITTLE JOHNNY LITTLEJOHN

"Time for your hot milk," the attendant said.

"Hot milk, hell!" the old man said. "Hot slop!"

"Big doings up Thurman way this afternoon," the attendant said.

"Hot whitewash!" the old man said. "I bet my shabby old ribs look like a picket-fence!"

"Seems the town wanted Dan Hunter to kick out some nigger-woman. . . ."

Half a glass of warm milk hit the attendant in the face. "By God in the sky!" the old man said. "I say the South *lost* that war!"

### TOM QUINN AND ELI BISHOP

Bishop said, "Aaron Platt, Doc Slocum, Gracie Paulhan, Dan Hunter, and the nigger-woman! I tell you, Tom, there ain't been no meal like it since The Last Supper!"

Quinn said, "Was Judas there too, Eli?"

131

"Judas?" Bishop said. "Judas who?"

"Judas," Quinn said. "Just plain Judas."

Bishop blew a parasol of smoke into the air. "I don't think I know the man, Tom," he said.

## ANSON AND DAVE UPDEGROVE

"Pop," Anson said, "what's a whoorhouse?"

"Don't be asking questions, son."

"I want to know," Anson said. "What's a whoorhouse?"

"Where'd you hear the word?"

"When I come past Polk's, Mister Bishop was saying the preacher spent half his time in a whoorhouse."

"I think you ought to take that puppy out of the parlor, son."

"What's a whoorhouse?"

"It's a place where men go sometimes."

"Do you go, Pop?"

"Yes, son—sometimes."

"What do you do there?"

"Oh. . . . things."

"Good things or bad things?"

"Come here, son."

The boy sat on his father's lap, and the puppy, nosing under the man's vest, found the warm cave of his armpit. It crawled in as far as it could go and went to sleep.

"Good things or bad things?" the boy said.

"I couldn't tell you, son," the man said. "I don't know."

132

### LELAND POLK AND EMERSON POLHEMUS

"If the house was mine, Emerson," Polk said, "I'd slap a dispossess-paper on that woman quick enough to leave the print hanging in the air."

"You ain't thinking so good," Polhemus said. "She pays her rent regular as you change your drawers, and that's once a month. Why should I kick her out?"

"Because if she stays, the church goes."

"Sure, but if the church goes, who goes with it?"

"How the hell do I know? Everybody, I guess."

"Think!" Polhemus said. "If the church goes, who goes with it?"

"You mean Dan?" Polk said.

### SAM AND EDNA PIRIE

"We ought to ship them all back to Africa," he said.

"Surprised you don't make them *swim* back," she said.

### MISS FINCH AND DOLLY PIPER

Miss Finch said, "I wouldn't set down to eat with no nigger around."

"No?" Dolly Piper said. "How about if she was waiting on you?"

"That's a nigger of a different color," Miss Finch said.

### HERB ESTES AND ELI BISHOP

Bishop said, "There was so damn much food on the table you had to look twice to take it all in."

"Me, I fed up to Ash Harned's," Estes said, "and I got a slab from a pork I'd swear was butchered for the Civil War and fried for the Spanish-American."

"They had chicken up to the whoorhouse."

"Chicken! Chicken, no less!"

"And a leg of mutton."

"Chicken *and* mutton! Good Christ!"

"Couple of green vegetables too," Bishop said.

"We had boiled whistleberries," Estes said.

"And sop and corn muffins."

"Christ Almighty!"

"And fruit salat."

"Damn!"

"And a white cake with chocolate frosting."

"*God* damn!"

"I say that's a meal fit for a king."

"I say that's a meal fit to give me a fit!"

"But whoors have to eat, Herb," Bishop said.

"Not on *my* money, they don't!" Estes said.

### JOEL CONFREY AND TRUBEE PELL

"Trubee," Confrey said, "for a man that put in seventeen years at Dannemora for manslaughter, you sure act peculiar."

"How so, Joel?" Pell said.

"Well, for one thing, you ain't never been up to the Widder's."

"Is that peculiar?"

"If I'd been cooped up as long as you, I'd go for

134

anything that had a way into it. I'd be horny as a parson."

"I knew a man like you once, Joel."

"You did? I'd like to meet him."

"Keep on sticking your bill in like a humming-bird, and you will."

"When, Trubee?"

"Any day, now. He's been dead seventeen years."

### SLOCUM QUINN AND ELI BISHOP

Below Bishop, who was sitting on the railing of Polk's porch, a group of children were choosing an 'it' for a game of run-sheep-run. They stood in a circle around Slocum Quinn, holding up their fists for her to rap at each syllable of her mumbo-jumbo.

"Ibbity bibbity sibbity sab," she said. "Ibbity bibbity canal-boat. Dictionary down the ferry. Out goes y-o-U!"

"I know a better way to choose," Bishop said.

Slocum paused and looked up at him, and the other children looked up too.

"Here's the way it starts," Bishop said. "Eeny meeny miney moe. . . ."

### CLARA PENROSE AND ELI BISHOP

"Hello, Clara," he said.

"Hello, Eli," she said.

"Where you headed?"

"Home."

135

"I'll walk you."

"How you feeling, Eli?"

"Two to a hill. And you, Clara?"

"Everything's fine, and my hair's laying smooth."

"Ever hear from that New York jewelry-man?" he said.

"No," she said. "He ain't wrote me yet."

"How long's it been?"

"Must be nine-ten months, now."

"That's too bad, Clara."

"Nothing bad about it. He just ain't much on writing."

"It don't take much writing on a postal-card."

"I'm expecting a real letter any day."

"It's too bad about Dan Hunter too," he said.

"Dan?" she said. "Why?"

"I sure hate to see one of the town bachelors taking up with a nigger."

"Get away from me, Eli! You couldn't say anything decent if it was to your own advantage!"

"So long, Clara," he said.

### ABEL AND SELMA FRENCH

Still dressed in their church-clothes, they had been sitting on their back porch for a long time, and for a long time neither of them had spoken into the seventh-day languor of the barnyard. Fowl dozed in the deep grass. A dog scratched himself in slow-motion. The man rocked his chair with drowsy precision.

136

"I been thinking," he said.

"What about, Abel?" she said.

"The name Doc Slocum hung onto that nigger."

"America Smith?"

"America Smith. It's starting to burn the life out of me."

"Why, Abel?"

"I'm understanding it, that's why. *America Smith*!"

"I think it's kind of pretty."

The man turned slowly to look at her, so slowly that the movement became a threatening gesture.

"Go inside, Selma," he said.

"It's nice out here," she said.

"Go inside!"

The woman rose. "But on Sunday afternoon, Abel?" she said. "Even on Sunday afternoon?"

"I got to get my mind off of that name," he said.

### ABRAHAM NOVINSKY AND ELI BISHOP

" 'Nigger,' " Bishop said. "How do you say that in *your* language, Abe?"

" 'Negro,' " Novinsky said. "How do you say it in *yours*, Eli?"

### LIZZIE CASS AND DECKY LOMAX

"You know what I'd do if I was black all over?" Decky said.

"What?" Lizzie said.

"I'd go keep house for Parson Dan."

"What about your father?"

"I wish I was black all over."

## MARK LOMAX AND ED SMEAD

"I been reading my Bible, Ed."

"That's a good thing to do on the Lord's Day—if you ain't married."

"I run across a piece in Leviticus that you ought to know about."

"How's it go, Mark?"

" 'Neither shalt thou lie with any beast to defile thyself therewith.' "

"Who said that?" Smead said.

"A feller name of God," Lomax said.

"Either you or God is getting almighty personal."

"Not with you, Ed."

"Who'd you have in mind?"

"Dan Hunter."

"I didn't know Dan was so scandalous hard up."

"He's keeping a nigger-woman in his house, ain't he?"

"What's that got to do with this Leviticus?"

"A nigger is a animal," Lomax said.

## JEFF BRANCH AND ELI BISHOP

Bishop watched a boy enter the drug-store and climb three feet off the floor to sit one of the iron stools in front of the soda-fountain.

"What'll you have, son?" Branch said.

"Please, Mister Branch," the boy said, "give me for a penny plain."

Branch set a tumbler of carbonated water on the counter, and the boy extended his fist across the sticky marble, but before relinquishing the penny he pleaded hard with his eyes.

"Please, Mister Branch," he said, "please could you squeeze in a drop of lemon?"

Branch smiled as he flavored the drink with a dash of syrup from one of the bottles that stood in a revolving rack. Delight broadened the boy's face, as if his remotest hope had been realized, and helping himself to a straw, he sucked up the bubbling yellow water. Finished, he sat still, staring at the wall. A burst of gas shivered his lips, and only then did the object of his visit to the drug-store seem to have been accomplished. He climbed down from the stool.

Branch let him reach the door before saying, "I'm giving away candy today, Sidney."

Belief bloomed slowly in the boy, like a picture on an inflating toy-balloon. He plastered his face against the glass candy-counter.

"Take your pick," Branch said.

"What's that over there?" the boy said.

"Lafayette mixture."

"And over there?"

"Mary Janes."

"And those long things?"

"Wax gum."

"I'll take. . . ."

"And these are candy bananas," Branch said.

"I'll take . . . ," the boy said, and then once more he hesitated. "I'll take. . . ."

Bishop pointed to a tray filled with glistening brown figures. "Why don't you take some of them nigger-babies?" he said.

### JEROME PIPER AND ELI BISHOP

Bishop sat on the river-bank, watching Piper's son Marvin flip plugs at the bass-pools below Thurman Bridge. Piper himself was working riffles some distance downstream.

"Marv," Bishop said, "what do you know about niggers?"

"Nothing, I guess," the boy said.

"You ever wonder about them?"

"Can't say I do."

"How's that, Marv?"

"Never seen any till this woman come to town."

"They're sure funny spessmens," Bishop said.

The boy switched pools and began to play one along the flank of a sunken log. Using a live minnow and casting with a made-over trout-pole, he stripped several coils of line and slung his bait across the channel. It fell a foot short of the aimed-for eddy, and quickly the current caught the slack in its teeth and ran. The minnow had almost been drawn into the drift when it was detained—detained, examined, and then suddenly taken

140

away on an up-river diagonal. The boy struck, but he struck early, and the head-half of the minnow sprang back at him with the relinquished line.

"Funny?" he said. "What's funny about them?"

"The way they're built," Bishop said.

"They're built from the ground up, far's I can see."

"That ain't too far."

"It's far enough."

"You take ordinary people, now," Bishop said, "they're built straight up and down. But you take niggers. . . ."

Stepping from stone to stone, the boy's father paused at the tackle-box for a change of plugs and continued upstream.

"Tell me, Eli," the boy said.

"Tell you what?"

"How're *niggers* built?"

Bishop grinned.

### ARISSA SECOR AND HANNAH HARNED

"What you got in that sack?" Hannah Harned said.

"A can of my preserve," Arissa Secor said.

"What kind?"

"Wild crab-apple."

"Where you carrying it to?"

"Gracie Paulhan's. Why?"

"Leland Polk'd give you fifteen cents for it."

"I can get more than that from Gracie."

"From the Widder?" Hannah Harned said. "Why, all she'd give you is 'Thanks'!"

"That's a sweet price," Arissa Secor said. "Leland couldn't meet it."

### BIGELOW VROOM AND ELI BISHOP

"Big," Bishop said, "how much Indian you got in your blood?"

"One-eighth Abenaki," Vroom said.

"How much would you have to have before you stopped calling yourself a white man?"

"I ain't white right now."

"Why, sure you are. You're only one-part Indian."

"Nope," Vroom said. "I'm only seven-parts white."

### PEARL HUSTIS AND CLEO BRANCH

Kneeling alongside her daughter's headstone, Pearl Hustis was planting a crawl of wandering-jew in the almost barren little mound. Only a few starts of grass appeared among the long-crisp death of earlier attempts to green the grave.

"Why can't I grow nothing here, Cleo?"

The other woman was looking at the breaker of vegetation that foamed over the parsonage fence. "I don't know, Pearl," she said. "Maybe you plant mean."

"I *feel* mean."

"Then you ought to quit trying to grow flowers."

"Anna Mae liked them."

"Anna Mae's dead, Pearl."

"She had green thumbs. She could grow grass on a stone floor."

"Can I say something, Pearl?"

"What, Cleo?"

"You're glad she's dead."

Pearl said nothing. She was reading the inscription on the headstone—ANNA MAE HUSTIS: born 10 April 1925, died 26 August 1939—and soundlessly her mouth added the word *Septicemia*.

"The women in this town," Cleo said, "they hate this America Smith because they've got to thinking that Dan Hunter's their own special man and married to every last one of them. You hate Anna Mae because when your husband laid with her, she turned out to be just another woman to you."

Cleo put her hand on Pearl's shoulder when she began to cry.

### HENRY MANSFIELD AND ELI BISHOP

"Hi, Hank."

"Hi, Eli."

"What you doing?"

"Setting," Mansfield said.

"Nice day for it," Bishop said.

"Setting and thinking."

"I never could do both."

"I been thinking about my dreams."

"I didn't know you done any dreaming, Hank."

"I'm always dreaming about the stuff in my store— sheets, pillow-cases, napkins, towels, stacks and stacks of them all piled neat and even. There ain't hardly nothing else in the dreams—only white-goods."

143

"I dream too," Bishop said.
"You do? What about?"
"Black-goods."


### ART HUSTIS AND ASH HARNED

Barely visible in the lilac evening, Bishop turned when he had crossed the bridge, waved once, and then continued on his way up Thurman road. A demijohn of applejack stood shoulder-deep between the two men lying in the long thick grass.

"Liquor does odd things to a man," Harned said.

"Ash," Hustis said, "you know what's a matter with this town?"

"Odd things. Look at Eli Bishop, now."

"I'll give you the answer: the people."

"One drink, and he's tighter'n a mink."

"The people! That's what's a matter!"

"One drink," Harned said, "and he's a goner."

"Town's fine, people punk," Hustis said.

"One drink, and he loses control of his feet."

"Punk, mister."

"Hate to say it, Art, but he loses control."

"Punk like in 'punkin.' "

"Loses all control."

"Punk like in 'punk.' Burn 'em, and you'd kill mosquitoes."

"Let him take one drink, understand, and he ain't got no more to say about where he's going than a dish of ice-cream at the Poor Home."

"If people was eggs, you couldn't find the bird that'd set on 'em."

"His shoes start walking, and he follows 'em."

"If people was cheese, rats'd starve."

"Don't make any difference where they go—he follows 'em."

"I don't even like *m'self*, Ash."

"Follows 'em to the nearest keyhole. I know, because I followed *him*."

"I'm going to tell you something, Ash," Hustis said. "You know what's a matter with this town?"

Harned hoisted the demijohn and took a long swig. "Oughtn't to admit it, but I *always* follow him."

"*The people!*" Hustis said, and then he drank too, making the mouth of the demijohn kiss the air as his lips came away. "You didn't follow him just now."

"Hell, I *seen* the nigger get undressed."

Hustis stood up. "People do the God-damnedest things," he said.

"That's what I been telling you," Harned said. "People're punk. Punk like in 'punkin.'"

### SARAH RITCHIE AND HELEN SMEAD

"Where's my Cora?" Sarah Ritchie said.

"She's in the house, Sarah," Helen Smead said. "She's playing with my Slocum."

"*Corah!*"

Through the screen-door came the sound of Cora's voice. "What's your *real* name, Slocum?"

"Pudden-tain," Slocum said. "Ask me again, and I'll tell you the same."

"What's your *real* name?"

"Jack Brown. Ask me again, and I'll knock you down."

"You ain't got no name."

"I have, too!"

"Then tell it."

"Slocum Quinn."

"*Slocum Quinn*! That ain't your name!"

"Who says so?"

"My ma says so. She says you ain't got no more name than that nigger-lady."

"I say my name is Slocum Smead Quinn!"

"My ma says you was born out of a wet lock, so you can't have no name."

"I was not born out of a wet lock!"

"You was!"

"I wasn't!"

"You was, too! You was born out of the wettest kind of a lock!"

Through the screen-door came the explosion of a palm against a cheek, followed, after a long moment of silence, by a spiral-staircase howl from Cora.

"I think Cora's ready to go home now," Helen Smead said.

## ART HUSTIS AND ELI BISHOP

"Eli, I want to ask you a question."

"Ask it, Art, but for Christ's sake, whisper!"

146

"Why? Can't you hear me when I talk?"

"*Whisper!*"

A lamp had entered the room they were watching, and giant shadows sparred with each other on the walls. Setting the lamp down, the woman began to unbutton her dress.

"I want to ask you a question."

Under her dress, the woman wore a white cotton slip.

"Are you ready for it, Eli?"

The woman took off her shoes and stockings.

"Here it comes, Eli."

The woman stood for a moment with her hands on the foot-board of the bed.

"I'll give you a hint. It starts with 'Why.' "

The woman blew out the lamp and finished undressing in darkness.

"Art," Bishop said as they stumbled down the hill, "you're so drunk you couldn't find your hat with both hands."

"I want to ask you a question, Eli."

"Ask it, and to hell with you."

"Why don't you get married?"

## GUS RITCHIE

A group of townsmen were gathered on Polk's porch, among them Ash Harned. It was shortly after nine o'clock in the evening.

"I wonder how Bishop and Hustis is making out," Harned said.

"I took a snooze this afternoon," Ritchie said, "and while I was snoozing, I had a dream."

"What did you dream?" Polk said.

"Dreamt God come and put His hand on my shoulder."

"Put His hand on your shoulder? That's bad, Gus."

"Put His hand on my shoulder and looked me straight in the eye."

"What did *you* do?"

"I put my hand on *His* shoulder," Ritchie said.

"Did you look Him straight in the eye?"

"Straight smack in the eye."

"Was He friendly?"

"He couldn't of been more so," Ritchie said.

"Did He say anything?" Polk said.

"He looked around, taking in the trees and houses and fields and people—specially the people—and He said, 'Gus, tell me the honest truth: did *I* do all this?' "

"And what did you say?"

"I said, 'That's what they tell me, Mister.' "

"And now God again?"

"He said, 'Gosh, Gus, I guess I didn't know my own strenkth.' "

☼

# GOD IN THE HANDS OF AN ANGRY SINNER

## 1741 A.D.

GOD: I just got around to reading the Holy Bible,
and I'm bound if it's worth a belch in a cyclone.
It hangs a whole slough of fancy names off of me,
like tin cans on a dog or like tails on a kite,
but if I'm a rag-tailed kite or a tin-canned dog,
it ought to tell how fast I run or how high I fly.
Starting out with only what I had in my pockets
(an agate that I'd swapped for a sack of marbles,
a piece of twine, a cold deck, and a front tooth,
also a bullfrog and four lickrish jaw-breakers),
I throwed this world together in six days flat,
after which, being winded, I kind of took my ease,
took it, I guess, for about six thousand years,
and never once, till I went and read that book,
did it dawn on me that all of you weisenheimers
had me figured as just another owly-eyed old coot
with nicotine on my burnsides and a gimpy leg.

149

That's got to stop, bub—every damn bit of it!
I ain't played out yet by one hell of a sight:
I'm God Almighty, and I want a little respect!

  *BUB: Squat, Mister, and rest your hands and face.*

I'm obligated, but if it's all the same to you,
I'll speak my mind while standing in my leather;
this game leg of mine is sure giving me grief,
and if I ever cock it alongside of a porch-post,
I couldn't shove myself back up together again. . . .
Now, bub, what's this about you laughing out loud
plumb in the middle of Preacher Edward's sermon?

  *It's as true as gospel, Mister, and maybe truer.*

If you hadn't of been such a tickle-toe, bub,
you might of heard something to your advantage.
All the time you was busting your belt in there,
he was trying to clap his main holt onto your soul,
saying, "Laugh if you like, laugh your pants off,
but by Myself, you're all going clean to hell!"
saying, "You're crows, you're locusts on the land,
you're slugs, you're bugs in bed, and beetles,
you're worms, and worse, you're the cast of worms,
you're snails, you're dung-hill flies, and ticks,
and by Me Almighty, you're all going clean to hell!"

  *Take it easy, Mister. It's a ruinating hot day.*

I'm about froze, but if you're letting off sweat,
it's hell you feel, and don't ever think it ain't.
The fire's creeping and crawling around the edges,

150

with three shifts of devils to huff and puff it,
and Old Scratch in person is licking on his chops,
and me, bub, I got a sword hanging over your head
sharp enough to slice water without getting wet.

*That's quite a tool, Mister, quite a cutting tool.*

It's the cuttingest damn tool you ever seen, bub,
and a skull wouldn't turn it no more than a pie:
I'm good and mad, but just get me *bad* and mad,
and you'll be two men with only half enough face.

*You're one hell of a hard guy, ain't you, Mister?*

Hard! Why, I chew Star Navy and spit ham gravy!

*I wouldn't chew, Mister, if I wore them plates.*

I'm God Almighty, bub, and I want some respect!

*Not so iron loud, Mister. You'll raise the dead.*

I done that before, bub, and I can do it again.

*Don't do it here, Mister. It's just been cleaned.*

It's been so long since you had any misery, bub,
that you've went and got big for your britches.
You're all swole out like breakfast in a snake,
and that head of yours is just aching for a rock.

*It's about time you stated your business, Mister.*

I'm fresh from stringing new wire all around hell,
and I seen the damnedest assortment of wiseacres
that Satan ever put through a course of sprouts.
There they was, every known kind of mortal man:

stout and lean, young and old, bald and bearded,
black, white, red, yellow, buff, and patch-work,
good, bad, and so-so, tight, loose, and in between,
horny-handed, lily-livered, pigeon-toed, and mean,
the rich and pimpled, the incestuous and devout,
the master of hounds and the mistress of whoors,
the running, the walking, and the standing still,
the pure and fornicating, and the sick and well—
there they was, bub, laying twelve-deep in grief,
with enough left over to make me an extra world,
and the screeching they let out when I went by,
the dying without death till the cows come home,
the blood, the sores, the thirst, and the pain,
it would of wrang the heart of anybody but a God.
So, bub, if you got anything to say for yourself
before you get fried in deep fat like a cruller,
if you got a prayer to make or a bribe to offer,
if you know you're damned, but want to be saved,
if you'll say 'Uncle' and eat a snootful of crow,
if you'll love me while I hate the sight of you,
if you'll kiss my foot while it tromps your face,
if you'll believe I'm good, and only man is evil,
if you'll believe I'm God and believe on your knees,
then bow down!

*Did you say bow down, Mister? I bow down never!*
*It'd take a pair of amputations to make me kneel,*
*because I'm a man, and while I work my joints,*
*I aim to stand up straight in the air, like you,*
*and not lick dust like some serpent so poisonous*

*that if it crossed the shadow of a flying bird,*
*the bird would break to flitters on the wing.*
*I'm a man, Mister, and I want a little respect!*

You're built out of beef, blood, and bone, bub,
and if you keep on begging to be hung on a hook,
I'm going to get splashed like a butcher's beard.

*Talk like that use to scare the wadding out of me*
*whenever I got a dose of hell for breaking Sunday*
*(meaning a psalm and a hot clout next to my jaw*
*from a old man that knowed how to handle hands*
*for two things only: psalm-singing and battery),*
*but there come a day, Mister, when I was fifteen,*
*and I guess the old man never seen me stripped*
*or he would of damn well let it go at preaching:*
*I took the cant, but I give back the buffets,*
*I give them back with interest, a dozen for one,*
*I beat the whey out of that old son-of-a-bitch,*
*and if I bust my hands busting his prat crossways,*
*he never doubled his fist again except to point.*

By whaling on your old man and horsing in church,
you gummed up two of my best commandments, bub.
I always been partial to the Fourth and the Fifth,
being a family man myself and liking my rest-day,
so when it comes to toting up your good and bad
and figuring if you're headed for Heaven or hell,
you won't have a chance.

*He never doubled his fist again except to point,*
*and he pointed, Mister, but it was mostly at rock*

*because that's just about all we had under fence.*
*If we could of sold it, we'd of been rich as sin,*
*or if we could of et it, we'd of got fat like you,*
*but it couldn't be et, and it couldn't be traded,*
*so we stayed porer than snakes trying to move it.*
*We moved it, Mister, we moved it stone by stone,*
*but where we dug one up, we only growed two more,*
*and finally my old man sat back on his religion,*
*saying, "The farm's yours, son, every acre of it,*
*and if you work hard, you'll strike dirt some day.*
*Me, I'm off to pray; it's too damn tough to plow."*
*God was my rock too, but if I ever prayed on Him,*
*if I ever bent my neck except to blow my nose,*
*if I ever salted Him with anything but hot sweat,*
*if I ever begged Him for so little as the time,*
*let Him take me apart at the seams, like a fowl,*
*Mister, let Him reel me in dead as a trout-fly!*

You're dead now, bub, but you're late laying down.

*If I ever hit dirt in this quarter-section, Mister,*
*it must of been what was blowed in from next-door.*
*I didn't have enough top-soil to fill a flower-pot,*
*and a crop just wore itself out crawling on gravel.*
*I got to be light-fingered about ground, Mister,*
*I got so I'd steal it by the pinch, like tobacco,*
*I'd never walk the road but what I loaded my hat,*
*and once in a while, to stuff some special crack,*
*I'd even rake it under the fence from a neighbor,*
*and thanks to such thievery, and also the wind,*
*I'd only come middle-age (meaning thirty, Mister)*

154

*when I actually had me a crust onto that quarry*
*that'd keep my seed from dribbling down to hell.*

What keeps *you* from dribbling is my almighty will.
I made you, bub, but I didn't give no guarantees,
and even if I did, yours wouldn't be worth a dime.
Take a last look around, and look anywhere but up.

*Mister, let's suppose we draw a bead on something:*
*do you clean out your ear-wax and listen for once,*
*or do I grab your pants and run you into the road?*

I'll listen, bub, but if you ain't got no complain,
I'll use the time to put a new edge on this blade.

*It don't make no neverminds what in hell you do*
*so long as you keep them threats in your pocket.*
*They don't turn a single hair of my head, Mister,*
*on account of after the kind of a life I've led,*
*there ain't nothing in your world can feaze me—*
*nothing, not you, Christ, the Devil, or the dark;*
*I've seen everything all of you could serve up,*
*and if I batted a eyelash, it was only at dust.*
*I stood up under enough work in my day, Mister,*
*to wear a span of bullocks down to their horns;*
*I worked knee-deep in rain and nose-deep in snow,*
*I got up in the dark and corked off in the dark,*
*and in between dark and dark, I coddled stones,*
*I give them suck, one by one, for something green,*
*and by all that's holy (meaning a stiff upper lip),*
*by God and by Jesus (meaning only a expression),*
*them stones of mine, Mister, they* did *come green!*

There's a man is falling a tree up the road, bub,
and I have to fix it so that he cracks his back,
also I've got seven-eight strokes to pass around,
and if I crowd it on, I know of a boy with fits. . . .

But if it was sour swink to get a stand started,
Mister, it was raw gall to bring it to its milk.
I got swamped in gumbo or strangled in powder,
but I misrecall having the right kind of a rain.
I don't mean every damn time, I wasn't any hog,
I mean once, Mister, I mean once in a whole life!
but with this God of mine, it was all or none,
it was a drought or another drown-you-out flood.
And when it wasn't water that addled my brains,
it was all the plain and fancy vermin on earth,
it was rats that got fat on corrosive sublimate,
it was ants that put away a cart-wheel overnight,
it was nits and gnats, it was fleas and flies,
it was weevils and weasels and wolves and wasps,
Mister, it was every pest under the sun and moon.
And when all of that three-ring plague was fed,
and when it wasn't weather that brung up bile,
what about Indians with bellies full of fire?
what about the teeth in the law, and the tithes?
what about high dreams of the neighbor's wife?
what about talking to sheep or talking to myself?
what about breaking stale bread with a stray dog?
what about reading my one book a hundred times
and knowing all its lies by a chapter and verse?

*What about it, hard guy? What about it, Rock?*
*If you're still listening, Mister, what about it?*

I'm listening, bub, and if you're all done ranting,
I want to say I honed such a blade on this sword
that you won't ever know you've been cut in half
till you start walking in two different directions.

*Is that all, Mister? Is that all you got to say?*

Oh, you could bust out with a bellow or two, bub,
just to get in the swing of what goes on in hell,
just to . . . say, why you taking your shirt off, bub?

*Say 'Mister' once, Mister . . . !*

Ain't you rolling up your underwear sleeves, bub?

*Say 'Mister' once, Mister . . . !*

What you expectorating on your calluses for, bub?

*Say 'Mister' once, Mister, and take to your heels!*

I'm God Almighty, bub, and I want a little respect!

*One, Mister . . . !*

You wouldn't pummel a sick old man, would you, bub?

*Two, Mister . . . !*

I've got a God of my own, bub, and he'd be sore.

*Three, Mister!*

Well, if it'll make you feel any better—'Mister.'

*Start traveling, bub!*

✿

157

# AT THE SCHOOLHOUSE

ON THE wall at the rear of the classroom, the hands of a clock were slowly perfecting the right angle of 9. The teacher, Tom Quinn, let his eyes rotate with the great second-hand, and again and again they toured the long-familiar numerals, but suddenly, as he completed one circuit and began another, he separated the shape of the figures from their arbitrary meaning, and once more, as when he was a child, only their postures seemed to explain them: the circumcized 1; the devout 2; the pugnacious 3; the servile 4; the pompous 5; the eavesdropping 6; the 7, the Peeping Tom of numbers; the 8, the female number; the 9, hat over heart, making a knee. . . .

The clock muffled nine hiccups. A boy standing under a belfry in the corridor yanked nine times on a dangling rope, and conversation in twenty mouths ran down with the running-down vibrations.

Quinn opened a note-book, and his finger shinnied

up a pole of twenty names. "Benjamin Pound," he said, "what was the cause of the Civil War?"

A boy rose from his desk and stared over Quinn's head at a lithograph of Custer and his men firing horse-pistols into a merry-go-round of Indians.

"You won't find the answer up there, Ben," Quinn said.

"*Dopey Benny*," someone said.

To the right of the lithograph hung an engraving of Farragut in the rigging of his flagship at Mobile Bay.

"Did you hear me, Ben?" Quinn said. "The Civil War."

"The Civil War . . .," the boy said. "The Civil War. . . ."

"That's right, Ben—the Civil War."

"It was caused by the South," the boy said.

"*Dopey Benny*," someone said.

"Is that all you can tell us?" Quinn said. "That it was caused by the South?"

Flanking the lithograph on the left was another engraving—Sergeant Jasper, at Fort Moultrie, snatching up the American standard as the split staff toppled.

The boy watched Quinn's hand, and as it picked up a pencil and moved toward writing a zero, he tried again. "The war was caused by the bombarᵇment on Fort Sumter," he said.

"Was that the real cause?"

"The real cause of what?"

"Of the war."

"What war, Mister Quinn?"

The pencil-point made a circle in the air half an inch behind Ben's name. "What war are we talking about, Ben?" Quinn said.

"I thought you said the Civil War."

"You thought right."

"Well, it was caused when they bombar<sup>b</sup>ed on Fort Sumter."

"Did they do anything else?"

The boy looked up at the front wall again, but Farragut was immobile at Mobile Bay, and Custer and Jasper told him nothing. He dove deep into his memory and came up blowing.

"The Emancimation Proclaplation!" he said.

Once more, this time in sing-song, someone said, "*Dop-ey Ben-ny, dop-ey Ben-ny . . .,*" and the boy clapped a hand up to the bee-sting of a BB on the back of his head.

Quinn smiled, saying, "There's somebody in this room whose teeth are going to pop like corn."

Forty shoes paused in the vacant moment, and the wind through forty lips rustled no whispers, but finally, in false-face, someone said, "*Dopey Benny!*"

"Sit down and pay attention, Ben," Quinn said, and the pencil-point landed near the boy's name, circled the field once, and took off again. "Thompson Kirby."

As Kirby stood up, one of his books fell to the floor. The boy seated opposite him hooked his foot around it and shuffled it away along the aisle like a puck.

"Yes, sir, Mister Quinn," the boy said.

"What's the right answer?"

160

"The Civil War was caused by John Brown."

"John Brown?" Quinn said. "What did he have to do with it?"

"He was a Nabolitionist," the boy said.

"What was an Abolitionist?"

"A Nabolitionist wanted to nabolish the Union."

"That's a new one on me, son," Quinn said. "Where'd you read it?"

"I didn't read it. I thought it up."

"You did? Well, sit down and forget it."

"It's the truth," the boy said.

"How do you know?"

"My father said so."

"You told me you thought the answer up yourself," Quinn said.

"He helped me."

"*Dopey Thompson,*" someone said.

"Just what did your father say?" Quinn said.

"He said there wouldn't of been no Civil War if it wasn't for the Nabolitionists."

"But the Abolitionists wanted to abolish slavery," Quinn said. "Was there anything wrong with that?"

"My father said that's all the niggers was good for—slavery."

"Is your father busy these days?"

"He's seeding," the boy said.

"He doesn't seed after dark, does he?"

"Nobody does."

"Tell him to drop in on me tonight," Quinn said. "I want to talk to him."

The boy stooped for his book, but it passed from foot to foot under cover of a blank and staring desk-high innocence. It was trapped for him by Aben Vroom.

Quinn chose another name from his note-book. "Marvin Piper," he said.

"What?" the boy said without rising.

"For one thing," Quinn said, "get up off your fat!"

"My foot hurts."

"Hold it in your hand, but stand up!"

Fake agony was borne with fake bravery as the boy jacked himself up from his seat.

"What was the cause of the Civil War?" Quinn said.

"It was caused by . . .," the boy said, and then he hesitated, and into the void floated a whispered word—*Secession*—a whispered whisper. "It was caused by Secession."

"What was Secession?" Quinn said.

The boy, waiting for a voice that never came, found himself facing plaster busts of Washington, Jefferson, and Lincoln that perched one-legged on a shelf like loons—all three crumby under a murrain of always settling soot.

"Secession was slavery," the boy said.

"How's your foot, Marv?" Quinn said.

"It ain't so bad now."

"Then sit down and listen with your clean ear. . . . Aben Vroom."

"*Dopey Aben*," someone said.

"Aben," Quinn said, "maybe you can help us out. What was the cause of the Civil War?"

"*Dopey Abenaki*," someone said.

"The Civil War was caused by States Rights," the boy said.

"I've been waiting a long time for those two words. Explain."

"*Dopenaki Abenaki*," someone said.

"Well, when this country was made up," the boy said, "the different states give up a lot of rights to the Fedral Goverment, and the Fedral Goverment let the states hold onto a lot of other rights, saying they would be held inviolent forever. . . ."

"*Abenaki Indian*," someone said.

". . . That was when there was only thirteen states," the boy said, "but pretty soon some more come along and wanted to join the Fedral Goverment. The North said, 'Okay, you can join if you haven't got no slaves.' The South got sore and said, 'That's what *you* say. Nothing doing without them slaves. . . .'"

"*Aben, the dog-eater*," someone said.

". . . They wrote out some compermises, but that didn't do much good because the South was always trying to get the bulge, and finally they got boiling mad and said, 'No more compermises. I guess we will stand on our rights and get out of the Fedral Goverment. . . .'"

"*Aben, the half-breed*," someone said.

". . . The North said, 'Nothing doing. When you come in the Fedral Goverment, you give up your right to get out.' The South said, 'How come, and who says so?' and the North said, 'We say so, and it's account

163

of the Consatution.' The South said, 'The Consatution is only a roll of paper, and we will tear off the part we don't like,' so they opened fire on Fort Sumter. . . ."

"*Aben is a red-skin son-of-an-Indian-bitch,*" someone said.

Marvin Piper sat across the aisle from the boy reciting, and two rows to the rear. Without turning, and speaking as if the words were part of his recitation, Aben said, "If Marv Piper don't quit, I'm going to do the same thing to him that Crazy Horse done to Custer."

The silence was pneumatic, the walls of the room resisting briefly an expanding balloon of silence, but briefly only, and freed, the balloon exploded.

Marvin rose so slowly to his feet that he seemed to be really in pain. "Say that again," he said.

Aben turned to him. "Pick on me once more," he said, "and I'll cut your heart out and eat it."

Quinn sat motionless as history replayed itself, and he remembered, while the fragment of time insisted: "'. . . I feel,' *wrote General Terry to General Sheridan, 'that our plan must have been successful had it been carried out, and I desire you to know the facts. In the action itself, so far as I can make out, Custer acted under a misapprehension. He thought, I am confident, that the Indians were running. For fear that they might get away, he attacked without getting all his men up and divided his command so that they were beaten in detail. . . .'*"

164

"If we wasn't in the classroom," Marvin said, "I'd spit in your eye."

"You ain't going to spit in my eye," Aben said. "Not here or no place else."

And Quinn remembered: "*. . . No, the Indians were not running. Flintlock, blunderbuss, and carbine had run them for three hundred years, from the Chesapeake flats, from the Catskill highlands, from the dunes of Kitty Hawk, from the Okeechobee swamps, and then cannonballs and promises had ferried them to the plains, and then Gold—and their backs were to the wall. But there were still some medals that Custer had not won, and there were still some commissions that he had not earned, and the Sioux were the only enemy the white man had on the continent, the only enemy to take the field, the only enemy to be killed for those medals and commissions—and Custer knew that. But the Indians were not running. They had run two thousand miles to escape the stick that spoke, but for once they too had Winchesters (never mind where they got them), and Gall and Two Moon and Crazy Horse were making their last stand—and Custer didn't know that. And when the last shot was fired, when the smoke had cleared away, when the Indians had gone, and the sun was going down, Custer stank as he rotted among other rotting corpses on the upshot ground of the valley of the Little Big Horn. . . .*"

"Why don't you walk over there and soak him one, Marv?" Ben Pound said.

"I'll mobilize him when school's out," Marvin said.

"Not if you're still yellow," Aben said.

"Listen, dog-eater," Marvin said, "say I'm yellow again, and I'll paste you one in the puss right here in this room!"

Quinn rose. "Don't be so fast with your pasting, Marv," he said as he went toward the two boys. "So you're the one who's been annoying everybody."

"What's it *to* you, Quinn?" Marvin said.

"A whole lot, boy. I can't call on anybody for a recitation without hearing your digs. If you're so good, why are you such a damned idiot when I call on *you*?"

"I ain't no damned idiot."

"Well, you're no wizard."

"I could bone up on all the slop you been teaching— only I don't feel like it."

"Why not?" Quinn said.

"You play favorites, that's why," the boy said.

"Who are they?"

"Abenaki, the dog-eater!"

"*Your* father's been talking too much with his mouth, too, Marv," Quinn said.

"He said your biggest favorite was a dog-eating Indian dog!"

"Tell your father I said he was a stupid liar, Marv."

"I'd sooner be a liar than a Indian."

"And while you're about it, you can tell him I gave you a zip for the week."

"You must be a Indian yourself," the boy said.

"I'm not an Indian, son, but now you flunk for the term."

"What for?" the boy said. "On account of the Indian snitched on me?"

Aben stalked him with his eyes. "I didn't snitch on you," he said. "I said my say to your face."

"I say you snitched! You want to make something out of it?"

"All day long," Aben said.

"You and what tribe?" Marvin said.

"Just me by myself."

"Say, do you know who you're getting snotty with?"

"Sure. With the yellowest white son-of-a-bitch in Warren County."

Marvin made a shell of his tongue and blew a clam of spit at Aben's face. It hit his temple, burst, and sidled down across his eyes, but before this and while the degradation was on its way, at some instant between the giving and the taking, between the dispatch and the delivery, Aben's one-sixteenth of Abenaki was trying to kill. Swinging his fist as if it held the handle of an obsidian axe, he sank it in the front of Marvin's face, and the boy's withdrawing tongue was caught between his hammered-shut teeth. They cut into it like chisels, and almost at once his face grew blood. Slowly, as if he had to verify with his touch what he had already tasted, Marvin put his fingers to his mouth; he looked at them and smeared the blood with his thumb; then he wiped his hand on the hip of his pants, slowly. He seemed suddenly, now, to grow taller, and he swayed, tottered a little, and then fell upon Aben rigidly, all in one piece, and it was as if a tree had come down upon a bush, a sledge upon a spike. Aben was crushed so quickly by the blow that he appeared to have been driven into the floor. For a moment he lay still, watching over-ripe berries of his blood break into blots on the dust of the floor. Then he propped himself, and his eyes were on a level with the compartment under his desk. In the compartment was a bone-handled barlow.

"Drop that knife!" Marvin said.

He tripped, retreating, and fell over backward. Aben jumped him like a monkey and rode his chest, and then a still-life from the Custer lithograph—an Ogallala poised over a fallen trooper—began once more to breathe. The barlow peeled a swatch from Marvin's skull, and Aben came up holding it like one skin from a fur-coat.

"Dopey Marvin," he said, and suddenly he slapped the fallen boy's face with the bleeding piece of himself.

✿

## THE MAN IN THE BLACK COAT

### 1775 A.D.

THEY remembered his act alone, because his name
(if there was a name) would have meant nothing,
but if acts without names are less than nothing,
call him Cato, like every second slave in pants,
or let it be Mingo, Salem, Primas, Sidon, Jubil,
or Corridon (if your taste runs to fancy handles),
or Quico, or Quaco, or Moody (which he was not),
or Barzillai (meaning *made of iron*, which he was),
or Cuff (a name given in love, you understand), or
let the name be London, for there were Londons,
let it be Scipio (major if large, minor if small),
let it be Pete, Andy, Jim, Jack, Phil, or Bart,
let it be Tom, Matt, Thad, Si, Jim again, or Jude
(aye, for Christ's sake, let it be apostolic!),
or anticipate history and make it Nat or Denmark.

But now that you've fixed the black and the slave,
and the nameless is named and the unknown known,

now that your Cato is no sullen shape in the mind,
but only a trick ape in a toy hat, a tile smile,
now (may I say?) that you're no longer afraid,
suppose you suppose the white name of his master:
suppose it to be Stribling, Dabney, or Slaughter,
suppose it Pepperrell (double *p*, *r*, *l*, Mister!),
suppose it Pickett or Moncure, Ruffin or Byrd,
suppose it Lynch of Lynchburg, suppose Dinwiddie,
or, since we're only supposing, suppose Washington.

*. . . There came, about the last day of August,*
*a Dutch man o' war that sold us twenty Negars.*

And one night he greased (as slaves called it),
he ran for it—toy hat, pants, name, and all.
Five times removed from one of those twenty Negars,
all his life a Virginian, yet knowing of Virginia
only what he could know by looking over a fence,
twenty-seven years old, yet never having lived
so much as one day that he could call his own
(but older than all things old beyond that fence
because of the endless adolescence of the slave),
unlettered from *a* to *z*, including the letter *X*,
six foot even, and thirteen stone (including hat),
colored like new-turned earth, condition prime,
and cash-value, on the hoof, two hundred pounds—
he greased one night, he took it at the double,
and when, hat in hand, the man in the black coat
spoke from the driveway up to the pillared porch,
saying, "I never would of figgered he'd run, suh;
he didn't look to me like the biggety kind, suh,"

the man on the porch (was it Slaughter or Pickett,
was it Penhallow, Cabell, Ambler, or Randolph?)
spoke down, saying, "I want him back, Mister!"

It was cold steel and hot lead against bare feet,
it was two dozen dogs against one sense of smell,
it was all the Old Dominion against one nothing,
but he was swimming the Chickahominy in the dark
long before the first fanfare of hound and horn.
Long? Make it a flat sixty minutes by the clock,
enough, though, for Tidewater to become Dahomey,
and therefore he swam not across or down, but up,
and a stunt never fobbed off on a cheesing baby
caught a man in a black coat with his pants down.
By the time those damn britches got disentangled,
night was over, and the rabbit was in his hole.

The day was forbidden time, and the one-way roads
led straight back across the muddy Chickahominy:
two footprints in the dust, and the jig was up,
and up, too, if there was fire or the ash of fire,
if the absence of a fowl was proved by a feather,
if fruits were picked and the wet cores found,
if a fish was eaten, and a single fin remained,
if shadows moved when there was no moving wind,
if a branch was broken, or if a rumor thrashed
from bush to bush, or if silent water splashed.

But no count was ever kept of the scuppernong,
or the frog, the nut, the berry, or the white slug
in the punk of fallen trees, or the honeycombs,

nor would any crib ever tell of a missing ear,
nor blades of grass that certain blades were gone,
and none would know of frost licked from leaves,
or of one egg less in some nest among the reeds.

There was no stopping, then, except for the sun,
and the second sun was rolling on the Pamunkey
when he went to earth—or better, went to water,
because all day long, till that second sun set,
he lived in it from his feet to his lower lip:
the birds, at first, were curious about a head
that floated like a dead bird in the river-grass,
but in their morning hunger they forgot the dead,
and once one came to perch upon its hair.

Another creeping barrage of the Chesapeake night,
and he put the Mattapony behind him, and miles,
and another, and he hit the Piscataway, but late
(a century after Bacon and an hour after dawn),
and day bagged him above ground and out of water.
He flattened where its opening salvo found him—
among the green arrested ripples of a vineyard—
and feet flattened the dirt a foot from his face
when a white man stopped to handle some grapes.
Close? He heard breakfast gurgling in white guts.

He left the vineyard, bombed by grapes of rain
that burst upon him night, day, and again night,
and he bucked in rain the grape-shot Rappahannock
to reach some hole in the ground, some haystack,
and the Potomac in rain, six rain-tufted miles

to stand (to soak) in sand warmer than the rain,
and the Patuxent (Maryland) in a plague of rain
that pocked the mud and then pocked the pocks—
a week of rain, a water-week to the Chesapeake
sun, then sun and navy-blue night to the Severn.

*How does he look now? Is he standing the gaff?*
*Has he lost weight? Does he feel up to snuff?*
*Are his clothes torn? Has he thorns in his toes?*
*Is he short of wind? Is he gray (Is he yellow?)?*
*Is he sorry he's free? Was it worth the trouble?*
*What does he think about? What's on his mind?*
*And for that matter, Mister, what's on yours—*
*catching him, maybe, and swapping for the reward,*
*or catching him, maybe, and maybe letting him go?*
*Is that it, Mister, or would you speed him along,*
*would you feed him, would you give him britches,*
*would you point out the way and tell him the names*
*of more northerly nigger-loving sons-of-bitches?*
*Why so lock-jawed, Mister? Why that faraway look?*
*Who do you think you are, Mister—Mister Christ?*

All he got from whites was the use of their earth,
and he got it because he had the feet to walk it,
not because some Jesus wrote him a quitclaim deed.
He made the Patapsco on black and African steam
(*ganted up, gimpy, picking thorns from his hair,*
*eating oats out of dung and the lice in his rags,*
*but a full inch taller than the fugitive slave*),
and he made the Back, Middle, Gunpowder, and Bush
on bark and beetles, on bay air and fallen leaves,

173

and the Susquehanna, yearning like a swimming dog
(*for the Chickahominy? for sow-belly and grits?*
*for a life-sentence on his knucks, like a chimp?*),
and the Elk (Little and Big), and the Brandywine
on the dandelion, on dung itself, and a dead dog
(*he's yellow, you understand, yard-wide yellow,*
*and if they ever caught him, he'd call it quits*
*after a go that only cost him a pair of arms*
*and a few minor injuries—one of them death*),
and the Delaware to Jersey, and Rancocas Creek,
and up the creek on cranberries (up for fair),
and on cranberry-cramps to the sand-struck pines,
and then down the old sea-floor sand to the sea
on nothing but the southeast wind (from Africa),
and now north in night to wade the Toms and wait,
with toes for bait, to claw some clawing crab,
and north on Manasquan clams, on sea-pickled fruit,
on shore-bird eggs, on fish-fins and fish-bones
from an osprey nest, on fish from osprey young,
on swamp-salt, swamp-water, and pistache slime,
north on what hands could lift and stomach hold:
and he was on the Hudson, on the Hudson palisade!
(*What does he think about? What's on his mind?*)

The flight entered its final and identical third,
to the River Charles: but shall more water flow
from the sky or flow under it upon New England?
Shall the water have names (the Thames or rain),
or shall it only be said there was no single mile

where feet could dry or spent sprung hair re-wind?
And shall more vermin be eaten and we determine
such trash from the mute testimony of its ash,
or shall it only be said there was no single meal
when hunger, the lingering illness, was stilled?

☼

Words were spoken, but the early-morning mist,
unbroken, hid those who spoke and him who heard
the shreds of words in the shredded-cotton air.
He listened, and the talk was of one christened
. . . let it be Pomp (for Pompey), let it be Zach,
or, because his face was black, make it Benajah,
let it be Crispus, Bristol, Titus, Tack, or Dan,
let it be Brittain or Jordan, Hallam or Epheram,
let it be a juggled name in a grape-vine legend,
let it be a name smuggled from the Chickahominy,
let it be letter after letter, spelling 'slave,'
but let these in this twisting mist be friends.

Let them be armed, let them have a gun to spare,
and powder, and let them share flints and lead,
let one of them surrender up a pair of drawers,
let them all embrace him, let them kiss his face,
let them break bread and marvel at his hunger
and shake their heads; make their bread shrink
and their smiles expand; make them make him eat,
and make them make sandals for his broken feet;
let them let him rest himself and tell his story

of the man in the black coat, and let them match
this Tory with another, but with a coat of red;
and let him let himself be led across the Charles
to a patch of ground, a mound called Bunker Hill,
and there, bound by the words, *"Don't fire until
you see the whites of their eyes,"* let him kill.

✿

# AROUND WARRENSBURG

### ABEN VROOM

ABEN was the only one in the class who did not follow Quinn as he took Marvin Piper to Doc Slocum's. He watched from the doorway until the troop had disappeared down the wooded road off Schoolhouse Hill; he watched, still holding the barlow in his right hand and the strip of scalp in his left. Looking around now at the disordered classroom—the fallen books, the forgotten lunches, the shoved-back seats, the blood on the floor, and the drip from an overturned inkwell—he quickly found its motionless but dominating core, its throne: the Custer lithograph.

As he stared at the picture, he remembered the words of a letter that his father had once read to him from a book:

"OUR GREAT FATHER AT WASHINGTON, ALL GREETING from the chiefs, braves, and headmen of your dutiful children, the Winnebagoes:
Father, we cannot see you. You are too far

away from us. We cannot speak to you. We will write to you, and, Father, we hope you will read our letter and answer us.

Father, some years ago when we had our homes on Turkey River, we had a school for our children, where many of them learned to read and write and work like white people, and we were happy.

Father, many years have passed away since our school was broken up, and our children are growing up in ignorance of those things that should render them industrious, prosperous, and happy, and we are sorry.

Father, it is our earnest wish to be so situated no longer. We would like our children taught the Christian religion, as before.

Father, as soon as you find a permanent home for us, will you not do this for us?

Father, this is our prayer. Will you not open your ears and heart to us, and write to us?"

The boy went up to a cork bulletin-board that hung directly below the picture. Holding the scalp up as if it were a notice, he nailed it home on the knife with an overhand plunge that sank the blade clear through the cork and into the plaster of the wall. Then, gathering his books, he spat effortlessly on the blood-stains in the aisle and left the classroom.

Instead of going home, he entered the woods, which were close to the school-yard and running away west, and started uphill along an intermittent creek. The water was still high, a yard-wide spill of it warbling down a staircase of boulders to flatten, here and there, into pools disturbed only by the transit of reflected clouds, by the trespass of an occasional bird that drank, bathed, and went away.

The boy stopped at one of these pools, took off his clothes, and went over to the edge; without waiting to test the water, he jumped in. For a moment, he felt as if he had exploded, and he lay destroyed in the water, grinning like a foetus. From a spot at the base of his neck, the cold smeared in all directions through his body, chilling his toes to pebbles, his fingernails to chips of frosted glass, his scrotum to a tight hard wrinkled purse. Reassembling himself, he bobbed on the surface, and after the cold of the brook, the cold air was as warm as steam.

He rose up navel-deep and slapped his body until it was rouged with palms and fingers, and then he climbed out of the pool and stood naked in the sun, turning now and then to feel everywhere the faint but pleasant irritation of drying. Overhead, as he dressed, the riveting-hammer of a woodpecker stuttered, and he caught chipmunks spying on him from rocks as big as haystacks, rocks held precisely in tiffany-settings of fern.

It was almost noon when the boy started down the hill toward home.

✿

He found his father sitting in the grape-arbor. Alongside the man, on an up-ended crate, were a copper oil-can, a few clean rags, and a clip of cartridges; in his hands he held a .38 Colt automatic, the barrel of which he was swabbing with a plug of oil-soaked silk. The boy held back a few feet away, but came on again to place himself within reach; as he waited for the man to pay attention to him, he idly hefted a bunch of unripe grapes.

"What're you ascared of, son?" the man said without looking up.

"I ain't ascared, pop."

"Then why're you creeping up on me like a Indian?"

"I *am* a Indian," the boy said.

The man raised his head now. "And a damn good one, they tell me," he said.

The boy jigged the fist of grapes on his palm. "Are you going to do anything to me, pop?"

"*Do* anything to you?" the man said.

"For what I done," the boy said. "Are you going to whale me?"

The man smiled. "The hell I am," he said. "Us Indians have gotten whaled enough."

The boy picked up the cartridge-clip, turned the cool smooth cocoon in his fingers, and then looked at the man.

"Us Indians have gotten whaled enough, son," the man said.

✿

## THE PIPERS' SON

Jerome Piper was working a team of horses and a plow in a roadside field when Marvin was brought home from Doc Slocum's by Tom Quinn. The procession had dwindled, but a few of the boys still dogged the event, fascinated by the distinction of bandages, and somewhere along the line of march Eli Bishop had fallen in. Piper leaned back against the reins and watched the approach.

"What the hell happened to *you*?" he said to his son.

"He got hung up on Aben Vroom," Quinn said.

"Aben Vroom!" Piper said. "What did the Indian use on him—a numbing-stick?"

"A knife," Quinn said.

"Why, the little redskin bastard!"

"Marv had it coming. He was breeding a scab on his nose all morning."

"Mister," Piper said, "take yourself to hell outside of that fence!"

"I will," Quinn said, "because that's where I belong. The fault was Marv's, and I intend to say so if this egg ever hatches."

Piper grabbed the long knotted dangle of rein from behind him and cut across Quinn's head with it as if it were a saber—across and back, across and back—and four broils appeared on the schoolmaster's face, one of them broken open and bleeding. Quinn reached down for a rock, but as he stooped he was slugged flat when one of the knots in the strap caught him on the mastoid-bone. Piper quit only when the horses took fright and dragged the plow away over the furrowed ground.

Bishop helped Quinn to his feet. "That egg's growed

to be quite a pullet," he said, and pointing Quinn at the road back to town, he gave him a nudge to start him on his way.

And now it was the horses that took a belting. Piper fought them to a stop, and then, anchoring them with the plow-point, he galled their rumps and stifles until they turned, their ears flat, and tried to climb him, and he was giving them whang-leather across the muzzles when Bishop took him by the switching-arm and hauled him off.

"Took a knife to my Marv!" Piper said. "A knife! What do you think of that? *Took a knife!*"

"Who took?" Bishop said, riding Piper's bucking arm. "Who took, you dumb son-of-a-bitch? *The horses?*"

"A knife! God damn it, *a knife!*"

"That's right—a knife," Bishop said, "but whose knife?"

"I'm going to kill that little Indian shitepoke! Watch me, and see if I don't kill him!"

"Here's your arm back," Bishop said, "and don't go ruining no more horse-flesh."

✿

## AT HENRY MANSFIELD'S

America Smith was the only customer in the dry-goods store. For a moment Mansfield watched her turn the pages of a pattern-book, and then he looked away, his eyes wandering over tables heaped with remnants, over stacked bolts of cloth, over his name spelled backward on the window, and settling, finally, in the settling lint above a rhomboid of sunlight at the door. The village was almost silent in the early afternoon. Leaves were flippant in an infrequent wind, and a car made a rapid tide of sound on the asphalt, but there was no other movement, and there were no voices. Mansfield's eyes went back over his reversed name, over the neat rolls of cloth, over the rummaged confusion of remnants, and America Smith was looking at him.

"Find anything you like?" he said.

"This," she said, pointing to one of the patterns in the book. "Number 526."

"526?" he said. "Is that the one with the puff sleeves and the cross-stitch work?"

"Yes," the woman said.

"You're the first ever called for it," he said, turning to a box of envelopes on the counter between them, "but me, I always fancied it had city-style." He ran his finger over the tops of the envelopes, took one out, and slapped it free of dust. "Number 526," he said. "Anything else?"

"I need some material."

"There's plenty to pick from," he said, and he waved a hand at his shelves. "Help yourself, and take your time."

The store was a world of textile odors, a graveyard of organisms embalmed by machine. The woven fibers of cotton, flax, silk, and wool—taken alive from a living plant, a living animal, a once-living insect—were dead here, and in death they attested not the sun and the earth and the always-living rain, but the inorganic loom. The dry-goods were dry.

The woman was standing at a pier-glass, with a drape of pale yellow muslin over one shoulder, when Sarah Ritchie and Hannah Harned entered the store.

"Hi, ladies," Mansfield said.

"Hi, Hank," Sarah Ritchie said. "I want a paper of pins for a nickel."

"I got a customer, Sarah."

"So I seen. Reach me them pins, and don't get funny."

"I said I got a customer. First come, first served."

"That rule don't go between whites and niggers. Do I get them pins, or not?"

Mansfield looked beyond her to the woman at the glass. "Made up your mind yet, Miss Smith?" he said.

"Yes, I have," she said, carrying the bolt of muslin to the counter. "I want this."

"How much of it, Miss?"

"Four yards, I guess."

"Better make it five if you want the skirt to be full," Mansfield said.

"I want a paper of pins for a nickel," Sarah Ritchie said.

"Nice color, ain't it?" Mansfield said, offering the end of the cloth to Hannah Harned. "You ladies know each other?"

"We met in church," Hannah Harned said.

184

"Holy ground—a good place to meet people," Mansfield said.

"I want a paper of pins for a nickel!"

"Remember how I tried to sell you Number 526 last time you was in, Sarah?" Mansfield said. "Miss Smith, here, she went and picked it out all by herself."

"Come on along, Sarah," Hannah Harned said.

"I want that paper of pins, Hank!"

Mansfield indicated to America Smith a glass-covered display of spooled thread: the colors were arranged in seven rows reading from left to right, each beginning with a raw and violent primary, and grading, from spool to spool, to the mildest water-wash, the palest fade on the shady side of white.

"There's every color but the one on God's tongue," Mansfield said, "and b'Jibs, I'd have *it* if it was on the market." He looked at Sarah Ritchie and Hannah Harned, saying, "Number 526 calls for a cross-stitch, and damn if there's anything prettier than a cross-stitch if you take the right colors."

America Smith removed two spools of floss from the display and set them down on her folded cut of muslin.

"Brown and green!" Mansfield said, slapping the edge of the counter. "Why, if you'd of asked me, b'Jubs, you couldn't of come closer! Green like leaves and grass, and brown like soil that never felt a plow—brown like your complexion, if you'll excuse the expression, ma'am." He turned to Sarah Ritchie. "Remember my recommend, Sarah? Brown and green, I said, brown and green like all outdoors."

"Hank, for the last time: do I get my paper of pins?"

Mansfield looked at her for a moment, and then he spoke. "*My* paper of pins," he said.

Sarah Ritchie and Hannah Harned, in shoes that spoke like stretching ropes, walked precisely toward the door. They walked precisely and rapidly, like sandpipers, but America Smith's voice stopped them like fright. "*Brown and green wouldn't have gone so well with her pimples.*" They walked precisely again, and rapidly, and out.

✿

America Smith was gathering her parcels and paper sacks and making ready to leave Mansfield's for the parsonage; she had put the largest package in the crook of her arm and was piling up the others when the storekeeper, who from time to time had been glancing at the window, detained her.

"I'd stick around for a while," he said.

"Why?" the woman said, continuing to pick up her purchases.

"It's going to rain."

"Part of Warrensburg's going to get wet."

"I didn't know you'd been watching, ma'am."

The road, deserted before, was hardly crowded now, yet even in the pie-slice of vision limited by Mansfield's window, several cars and one-horse rigs were drawn up along the fringe of the pavement, and here and there a driver or a passenger had climbed down to lean back against a wheel or a fender, and here and there too a townsman had come up to join them in their silence. With talk free, the gathering would have looked like a section of spectators much too early for a parade, but there was little sound except for the stomp of a hoof on gravel, an occasional greeting, and once a series of barks suddenly begun and suddenly ended.

Mansfield opened the door for America Smith and followed her outside. The line-up of vehicles and loungers extended, with one clear break, for some distance up the road. The vacancy was the one-hundred-foot strip of asphalt fronting the property of Bigelow Vroom.

"It's going to rain," Mansfield said. "Yes, ma'am, it's going to rain puppy-dogs and saw-logs."

The sun rebounded from the road in shivers of hot air, and starts of wind sent up dervishes of dust that spun briefly and collapsed. America Smith nodded to Mansfield, and leaving him in his doorway, she went down into the road and started for home. As she passed the first of the parked cars, a man crucified to the spare tire dropped a comet of brown spit near her feet, and then, as more cars and more people were left behind, a droning swarm of whispers rose.

The woman reached the clearing in the road at the same time as a party coming from the opposite direction, a party composed of Jerome Piper, Marvin, and Eli Bishop. She gave her share to the right, but the trio crowded her, and instead of avoiding them, she came to a stop.

"Nigger," Piper said, "get to hell out of our way!"

and waiting for neither reply nor obedience, he batted her pile of packages into the air; the one containing the muslin fell near the roadside, skated over the gravel margin, and wound up in the cocoa mud of a ditch.

Bigelow Vroom stood cross-ankled against the newel-post of his stoop. On the steps alongside him sat Doc Slocum, Aben, Tom Quinn, and Dan Hunter. Hunter, from within, and Piper, from without, started for the gate at the same time, but Hunter reached it first, went through, and closed it behind him, saying nothing as he brushed past Piper on his way to help the woman recover her packages.

Piper's hand was shooting the gate-latch when Bigelow Vroom, still buttressing the post, spoke to him. "Don't open it, Jerry," he said.

The four words were not conversation: they were words, and they had been uttered, but they were all meaning, undressed of command, query, or warning; they were pure fact; they were a lock on the gate, and there was no key to that lock in any possible reply that Piper could have made, but he tried to fit one from the always-ready ring of talk.

"I want that boy of yours, Bigelow."

"So do I, Jerry, and I've got eight shots and then a gun-butt to keep him with."

"He used a knife on my Marvin!"

"And if the shots miss, and the gun comes apart, I'll still have another thirty years to brain you from behind some bush."

"He's a criminal!"

"And in thirty years, Jerry, I'll sure as hell find me that bush."

Vroom took his right hand from the pocket of his coat, and as he pointed the fat black finger of the gun-barrel at Piper's belly, his thumb threw the safety, and he said, "You can come in now, Jerry."

Piper murdered him with his eyes: he walked up to him with a 12-gauge shotgun and blew both of his lungs out through his back; he shoved a bowie into his navel and opened him as if he were entering a tent; he choked him until his tongue hung like that of a pistoled horse. But in the end, Piper turned away, slammed his hat on the ground, and swore, swore hard but aimlessly, and then, looking up, he saw Hunter retrieving the package from the mud. "Son-of-a-bitch," he said, "there wouldn't of been none of this if our preacher wasn't laying up with a nigger whoor."

Hunter removed the soaked paper from the package and threw it away. Handing the stained material to America Smith, he slowly and thoroughly dried his hands on a handkerchief, and then, with the secure ease of one knowing that only he could thaw out the tableau, he went to the nearest buggy and drew a whip from its socket, a whip made of braided cord and finished off with lacquer. He held the lash down as he walked toward Piper, saying, " 'A fool's lips enter into contention, and his mouth calleth for strokes.' "

"*Laying up with a nigger* . . . !" Piper said as he tried to fade.

Hunter sewed the man's face shut with one slashing

stitch across the mouth, but he was looking now, as before he swung, at Eli Bishop. Bishop did not fade. He held his piece of open ground near Vroom's fence and waited for Hunter's move.

"Eli," Hunter said, "I don't like Jerry Piper—I never did—but the worst fault he has is that his tongue is slung in the middle, and around it goes like a paddle-wheel. You're the one that spins it."

Bishop did not turn when Vroom came down to the gate and spoke to him over his shoulder, saying, "Don't run, Eli. I got something in my hand can outspeed you."

"I ain't running, Bigelow."

"I warned you once," Hunter said. "I warned you not to start any more stories going about preachers."

"The one you warned me about happened to be true," Bishop said.

"Maybe," Hunter said, "but the one I'm going to beat on you for is a lie."

"Maybe," Bishop said.

Hunter raised the whip, and it trembled overhead like a tassel of grain, but once more in an encounter with Bishop he experienced the sensation of a flowering mid-way between his belly-button and his back-bone, a seed of emotion mounting so quickly toward blossom that the cycle, ending in death, would be complete in another instant.

"Don't run, Eli," Vroom said.

"I ain't running."

Hunter let the whip fall, saying, " 'A fool's mouth

calleth for strokes,' but what shall be done to you, who are not a fool? How shall the mouths of the wise be punished?" and turning away, he took America Smith by the arm and walked her up the road through the silent crowd.

"*I* ain't running," Bishop said.

✿

### AT THE PARSONAGE

Sitting on the porch, Slocum, Platt, and Hunter watched the early-evening wind skip across the now lavender surface of the pond; on the steps, in the after-glow vague against the shrubbery below her, sat America Smith. Silently a fish broke water, and loudly, like a slapping hand, it broke back; the utterances of frogs needed oiling, and the wings of crickets; and fireflies were moving stop-lights in the accumulating gloom.

" 'A fool's lips enter into contention,' " Hunter said, and the word *contention* rebounded so softly from beyond the pond that it was like a brush passing through hair, " 'and his mouth calleth for strokes'—but how shall the mouths of the wise be punished?" and *punished* too was a brush brushing hair.

"If that was me this afternoon, Dan," Platt said, "I'd of belted Bishop to death."

"Would you, Aaron?"

"Belted him to death, b'Jucks, and then made such a mush out of his carcass that the devil couldn't of handled it with a fork."

"You don't look it."

"Don't I?"

"You haven't got the face for it."

"I let Tom Paulhan starve dead as a nit right in my barn."

"That was a long jump from killing him."

"Not so's Warrensburg would know it: the town figures I fixed Tom as good as I would of with a double-bitted axe."

"But what do *you* think, Aaron?"

Platt rolled himself a cigarette before answering. "Do I think I killed Tom?" he said as he lit the spill. "Sometimes, yes; sometimes, no: it's hard to tell the difference between watching a man starve and cutting his throat."

"Why *didn't* you cut his throat, then? You hated him, and you wanted him to die. Why did you wait five days for God to do something that you could've done in five seconds? Why did you let God start the whole machinery of Heaven when all you had to do was open a knife?"

"If God was inside of that barn for five days, He'd of starved to death Himself."

"He was inside of *you*."

"He must of been a sight when He crawled out."

Slocum whittled a plug of tobacco into the palm of his hand and crumbled the shavings to splinters. "A certain woman came to Warrensburg a little ways back," he said, "and from that time to this, a certain man's been dead set on driving her out again. The dispute started off slow, but it's been picking up speed by the minute, and every grown-up and whistle-britches in the town's been sucked into it on one side or the other, like all of us went and fell into a cream-separator." He brought a match off his heel like an uppercut, but before touching it to his pipe, he looked at Platt and Hunter, their faces saffron in the flare. "We could've brought this up short once with a salve, a psalm, or a statute, but now it's moving too fast for the Penal Code, the Prayer Book, and the whole U. S. Pharmacopœia rolled into one."

"Aaron's for battery, blood, and death," Hunter said. "What're you for, Doc?"

"You kill a man," Slocum said, "and he sprouts wings before he's hard. People forget he was a no-good son-of-a-bitch to his brother, but they remember he was never seen to kick a dog—and, by God, before you know it, he's got defenders. I wouldn't *kill* Eli, but along with four-five others, I'd lay for him some night when he was coming home from a hunk of Lake George ginch, and I'd scare him all to smack."

Hunter said, "How about wearing masks so that he'd never know who wet his powder, Doc?"

"It'd be a neat touch."

"And if the whipping didn't shut him up, the next time you'd heat some tar. Is that right? And if the tar didn't do the trick, then you'd hang him so high the crows'd roost in his ears. Is that what you're recommending, Doc?"

"It wouldn't ever come to that, Dan."

"It would, man—just as sure as Jesus bled. If a boy

193

took to climbing trees, and you wanted to save him a busted collar-bone, you'd give him a cuff or two and a penny for lickrish, and the chances are he'd stay on the ground. But you can't cuff *Bishop* into staying on the ground without being ready to hang him if the cuffing don't take."

"Why not, Dan?"

"A boy's full of sap and struggle, but there's no evil in him except what he reads off the wall of a depot."

"Maybe so, but you don't cure that evil with a coat of whitewash."

"How do you cure it, Doc? Do you dynamite the depot, or do you take it apart board-by-board and nail-by-nail? Aaron's practical and quick, and you're scientific and slow, but either way it boils down to the death of a man named Bishop. To kill! Why do we always want to kill?"

"It's good for what ails you," Slocum said.

"Is everybody sick? Are you sick? is Aaron? am I? This book, here—is that all it's about? 1322 pages of Death?"

"Look up your Concordance some time. In mine, there are 66 lines devoted to Life and 123 to Death."

"I'll eat the book dry if there aren't four times as many references to Death in Gray's 'Anatomy.' "

"Four!" Slocum said. "Make it *forty*-four! Death's the only thing that's in it, but I have a livelier trade than you because I keep my book under glass, and you put yours in every pew. You sell something you call Eternal Life, but it comes in a plain wrapper and without coupons, so I beat you all hollow with the same product under a different name: Health. We're both fakers, though. We're both cashing in on Death."

"That doesn't mean we're in favor of it. I'd sooner preach at a wedding than a funeral, and you'd sooner set a bone than break it."

"That depends on whose bone it is."

"You can't kill a man for talking, and so far that's all Eli's done. I've ignored him, insulted him, and threatened him, and finally, this afternoon, I raised my hand against him—but he was still only talking when I turned my back and walked away."

"You *shouldn't* have walked away, Dan."

"What in God's name *should* I have done? Should I have swatted him once? twice? forty times? Should I have beat him to his knees, or got down on my own? Should I have called on God to smite him, or should I have done it myself? Should I have prayed or cursed? begged or commanded? given in or killed him? I want to know, Doc, because I've got to make the choice!"

"You should've made it this afternoon."

"I couldn't. I couldn't convince myself that he'd done enough."

"How much would he have to do, Dan?"

"He'd have to do more than talk."

"He'll never do more than talk."

"I'm satisfied if he stops at talk," Hunter said. " 'Blessed are ye, when men shall revile you, and persecute you, and shall say all manner of evil against you falsely.' "

"If that's blessed, Dan, I'm damned!"

Platt shot his cigarette-butt over the railing, and it spun through its red-hot arc like one of the fireflies falling. "That's a pretty speech, Dan," he said. "Where's it come from?"

"Matthew."

"As pretty a string of words as man ever harnessed together—big flat-boned stock with fine hock-action. The only trouble is, they're so busy tugging in the wrong direction they couldn't pull a baby-buggy off a block of ice: it ain't what Eli said about *me* that'd raise my hackles; it's what he said about somebody else. Like Miss Smith, for instance."

"Aaron puts it, Dan," Slocum said. "As far as you're concerned, you can be as humble as God's poor relatives, but the minute you meech for another person, I'm ready to think sermons can be run up better by machine."

"Twist me one of those home-mades, will you, Aaron?" Hunter said, and for a moment he listened to the sounds of the process: the granular patter of pouring tobacco, the rice-paper rustle, the match-head rasp, and the fat-frying fire. "Thanks, Aaron," he said, taking the lighted cigarette. "Not even these can be made better by machine."

"You know who learned me?" Platt said. "A whoor."

"You learned it the hard way," Slocum said.

"Everybody learns the hard way," Hunter said.

"Everybody but Eli Bishop," Platt said.

"Even Eli."

196

"Hell, Dan, he's going to die in his sleep at ninety-five, with his hand on some wet-nurse's titty."

"God'll catch him in His own good time."

"With the head-start God's giving, He'll be twelve miles back at Judgment Day."

"God don't have the foot He used to have," Slocum said. "In the good days, He could hustle like Dan Patch driven by Old Scratch. Right now, He couldn't run downhill if He was water."

Hunter took a long deep suck on his cigarette and blew smoke in a long slow stream at the spark. "Do you think I was meeching this afternoon, Doc?" he said.

"This afternoon is over."

"Do you think I'm meeching now?"

"Well, Dan, you're doing something I've never seen you do before: you're falling back on a book two thousand years dead."

"Two thousand years *old*, Doc."

"Dead, Dan—so dead that it's stopped decaying."

"Sleep isn't death."

"A snooze like the Bible took today would've fooled an embalmer."

"Eli Bishop wasn't fooled. When I picked up that whip, I meant to kill him, and he knew it."

"If you meant to kill him, you'd have done it with two hands, ten fingers, and six quarts of hot blood. When you picked up the whip, we all could've gone home: it showed you'd been thinking."

"I *was* thinking," Hunter said, and a voice said *inking* across the pond. "I was thinking: 'Now he can breathe, and walk, and speak, and spit, but in another moment his breathing, walking, speaking, and spitting will be things I'll have to try hard to remember, and one by one the facts of his face will dwindle, and the day will come when I quarrel mildly about the spelling of his name, and then the name itself, even the name, will be forgotten.' That's what I was thinking, Doc: that death comes once, and it stays."

"God's been doing it every day for years."

"I was thinking: 'Death wears like iron—one of them'll last a man a lifetime.' "

"Think what *God's* got on *His* conscience."

"I'm not God! Damn it, man, I'm not God!"

"I never thought you were, Dan."

"Am I supposed to kill because God does?"

"Look," Slocum said, "you're not supposed to do anything. You asked for advice, and we showed you some. You looked it over, and not liking it, you handed it back. That leaves us where we started—with you still asking, and us still knowing."

"Dan," Platt said, "where'd you get the notion there's a duty on you that ain't on us too?"

"I'm pastor of this bunch of witches."

"And all us dirt-farmers and doctors have to do is sit by and suck hay?"

"I'll handle Bishop, and I'll handle him the way I see fit."

"I thought God was going to have a finger in it."

"He'll have His whole arm in it."

"Excuse me for making small of your friend," Slocum said, "but I don't think He knows what's going on in Warrensburg, and if He does know, I don't believe He'll turn a hair to stop the town from shooting down to hell on a slack afternoon: He's only got two hands, and I'll bet my little black bag He wishes we'd quit running to Him with every damn skinned knee and bloody nose in creation. We've got a faceful of teeth and a handful of short hair, and being men, we oughtn't to rattle around in our britches like boys on Hallowe'en. All we own is this ball of mud we live on, and even though most of it's so poor you couldn't raise a rumpus on it with a keg of liquor, we aim to make it do the best it can while we're around to see it—and if some bastard gets in our way when God's out, then it's up to the rest of us to play God till God gets back. If you can't find that in your Bible, Dan, it's a long and fancy book about nothing."

"I'm a shepherd—not a hangman!"

"You're the first shepherd that ever fed a sheep-dog mutton," Slocum said, and he rose now. "Coming, Aaron?"

"If Dan ain't got nothing more to say," Platt said, and for a moment he suspended the rocking of his chair, but Hunter remained silent, and as Platt rose too, the chair, for another moment, rocked itself. "Night, Dan," he said, following Slocum to the steps. "Night, Miss Smith."

There were uneven footsteps on wood, gravel, grass, and dirt, and on the dirt, with an occasional tattered phrase, they diminished downhill and were gone.

✿

## THE BLUE AND THE GRAY—
## AND THE BLACK

### 1863 A.D.

DEAR JOE: By the time this letter reaches you
(the paper's wrinkled, and the smears are mud,
or blood, and I ask you to overlook the trifle
that I use a pencil: a spent soldier's stifle
is my desk outdoors here in the atomized rain),
I'll be a spy. When the sun sets by the clock,
I'll take off blue rags queerly faded to gray,
and give away my Colt and my condemned carbine
and wearing what I wore when I enlisted (rags),
I'll be crawling between two pickets into Dixie.

If I'm lucky, I'll still be crawling at sunrise.
If I'm not, I'll be a long time dying, and, dead,
I'll be lying not in some frugal loaf of earth
for quavering pilgrims to vault the bulge I make
and sink salt flavoring to my skull—Jesus, no!
I'll be taken apart inch by inch, like a snake,

and when the last inch jerks for the last time,
I'll be left to rot, and the devil-grass
(please forgive me this blasphemy of names)
will come to revel among a few forgotten bones.

I tell you of the danger not because I'm brave
and making small of it; I simply want to speak
before I die, to say that this, *this*, was why
I showed my hand when a show of hands was made:
it was not enough to sulk when sold for calico,
beads, and drink, or to maim or take our lives,
or to kill for the sweet favor of being killed;
it was not enough to plot rebellion, or to rebel
and be smoked like a ham or shot like a pigeon;
it was not enough to get religion second-hand
from some back-porch, and, praising Gawdamighty,
understand that only He made only you a slave;
it was not enough to take freedom-papers after
forty years in burlap and forty years of beans;
it was not enough to run away from the sad music
and the sadder laughter, and own your own mouth
while one acre of the South remained to nullify
its voice; and now and finally it is not enough
that I return with iron if I lie on the fringe
and send lead envoys in. I go in myself, Joe,
I go on my belly, stalking, but if I'm caught,
I beg you not to think I'll be that black snake
wrought into a jelly: I'll be like an Injun—
I'll be walking, Joe. . . .

✿

# AT POLK'S STORE

I⊤ ᴡᴀꜱ Saturday evening, and drawn up in front of the store was a rank of cars, trucks, wagons, and one-horse rigs from outlying parts of the township. At the counters inside, several people were picking over and selecting merchandise, and others, having collected a stack of cartons and bottles, were waiting for Polk to reach them. There was only one lounger: Bishop sat tilted back against a rack of fruit-crates.

". . . That comes to four-eighty, Mark," Polk said to Lomax. "Anything else?"

"Gallon of coal-oil," Lomax said, shoving a can across the counter. "And make it a gallon."

"I charge for a gallon, Mister, and I give a gallon," Polk said as he hung the can on the spigot of an iron barrel. "It couldn't come out evener if I used a eye-dropper."

When the can was planked down before him, Lomax hefted it, saying, "Some day I'm going to find out what a gallon weighs, and then you and me'll have fun."

"Shoot, let's have fun right now."

"I don't trust your scales."

"You wouldn't trust hell to be hot: you'll have to see for yourself."

"How much I owe you?" Lomax said.

"A five-dollar bill, and make it a five," Polk said. "Who's next?"

Polhemus hooked an arm around a neat building of boxes and jars and slid it down the counter toward the cash-register.

"What's it come to, Emerson?" Polk said, watching Lomax leave the store.

Polhemus put four bills and a coin on the counter. "I make it a dime over eight dollars," he said.

Polk rang up the sale. "That apple you're eating is on the house," he said, "but the one in your pocket goes on next week's bill."

"Clean forgot about it," Polhemus said. "Measure me out a gallon of coal-oil before I forget that too."

"Where's the can?"

"I'll just loan one off of you, Leland."

Polk drew a gallon of kerosene into a store-can, and Polhemus, with the can in one arm and his packages in the other, was on his way to the door when Polk said, "That oil's twenty cents, Emerson, and don't ever think it ain't."

"Clean forgot about it," Polhemus said, coming back to pay.

As Polhemus went out, Bishop said, "Nice trade you worked up, Leland."

"Listen, Mister," Polk said, "if God Himself come in here, He'd try to jew me." He picked up an egg-beater that Abe Novinsky had set on the counter. "This yours, Abe?"

"It will be after I pay for it," Novinsky said.

"And not a minute sooner, b'Jesus," Polk said. "Half a dollar takes it away."

Novinsky bounced a coin on the linoleum. "Now, I want you to do me a favor, Leland," he said. "Shove the egg-beater up your ass and then turn the crank till I come back!"

"What're *you* in a tizzy about?"

"That remark you just made."

"Hell, I didn't mean it personal."

"I took it personal."

"Oh, fiddle-faddle!" Polk said. "I'm closing for the night. Another Saturday like this, and I'll give the store away for six bottle-caps and a jaw-breaker."

Jerome Piper bashed down an empty can. "You can close up and pull the sidewalk in after you, but not till I get me a gallon of coal-oil."

"God damn the man that invented coal-oil!" Polk said. "I've sold a barrel of it in the past two hours, and all I've got to show for it's a pain in the ass!"

"Why don't you take out that egg-beater, Leland?" Bishop said.

✿

At Slocum's direction, Hunter broke the lamp-glare by pinning a towel to the bottom of the shade. Slocum himself was sitting in a chair at the bedside and timing with an old roman-numbered watch a pulse that had flagged in an hour from forty-five to the minute to an irregular thirty-seven. He glanced away for a moment to feel without counting, and on the wall at the foot of the bed he saw the Sharps carbine, its woodwork polished now and its metal gleaming.

It was nine o'clock in the evening, and Little Johnny Littlejohn was dying.

✿

## PATTERN NUMBER 526

Light came from the eyes and mouth of Bishop's kitchen: the two windows and a crack under the door between them. The woman paused on the top flagstone of the stoop, and then, opening the door without knocking, she found Bishop sitting sideways to a table in a northeast-southwest slash of lamp-shine.

"I came to tell you something," she said.

He saw her first as a dress hanging in the doorway. *The dress was tight-belted, like an egg-cup.*

"I came to tell you my thoughts."

"Tell," he said, looking at the dress.

"I thought of going away," she said, "I thought of walking out of Warrensburg and never coming back, as if there were no town between the two iron bridges, no houses along the road, no people in the fields, no dogs, and no shade, but I knew that wherever I went I would always be in a place that would make me think of leaving it because there was nothing to stay for; I knew that I would always be in Warrensburg."

*Deployed in a hollow square at the edge of the high square throat, a line of cross-stitches sprawled like riflemen.*

"I thought of sitting still on the steps of the parsonage and waiting for Dan Hunter to stop rocking and stand up, but I knew that he would never stand up before God stood him, and I knew that even then he would be all talk and no hands."

*The sleeves fell full to overhang the cuffs, and on the cuffs too pickets of crosses lay prone.*

"I thought of kneeling down and praying a prayer for Dan's God to stand up, but I knew that if God's Dan was still rocking, Dan's God would still be rocking too, and I knew that God was all talk and no hands."

*Pleated at the neck-line and pleated at the waist, the loose and blooming blouse was blank yellow muslin.*

"I thought of making the law stand up, but I knew that the law would never stand up by itself, that it was only a suit of clothes people were allowed to wear if they were white, and I knew that the law too was all talk and no hands."

*From the waist, the skirt swept like a sweeping broom, and here and there, as if spun up from the floor, a solitary cross tumbled among the folds.*

"I thought, finally, of standing up myself."

"You made a good pick," Bishop said, and he turned the lamp down until only a blue caterpillar of fire rippled on the wick.

"I thought that if I told you my thoughts, you would stop thinking of me as something on a mattress, or in a ditch, or backed up against a wall."

In an empty instant, Bishop stared at one of the crosses that spattered the woman's skirt. "You fooled me, nigger," he said.

"I thought that if my words were good enough, they would make you understand what you would never understand from whips."

"I don't like to be fooled."

"I thought you would understand the one thing that makes us different and the many things that make us the same: my face is black to you, and your face is white to me, but to both of us all grass everywhere is green."

Bishop went to a window and pulled the shade down to the sill, and now the room was blind in one eye.

"I thought you would understand that only in the case of people do people think about color."

Bishop drew the shade over the other window, and now the grinning room was sightless.

"I thought that no man would go barefoot if his only shoes were black. I thought that he would drink black tea and black coffee, and that if he was hungry he would eat black bread and blacker meat. I thought that he would listen to a preacher in a black suit and take his hat off to a nun's black gown. I thought that he would read black print, and write with a black pencil, and put his white mouth on the black mouth of a telephone. I thought that he would want black earth above all other kinds of earth. I thought that he would never wash but what the water darkened, nor ever build a fire but what it ended in black ash. I thought that when night came, he would sleep in a black room, and I thought that when death came, black horses would pull a black hearse to a black grave. I thought that he would laugh himself black in the face at a comedian in burnt cork—but when, I thought, when would the black tragedy of being black without burnt cork bleed his heart white?"

Bishop closed the door behind the woman, and then even the grin was gone. "Niggers shouldn't fool around," he said.

"I thought that all these things would be good things to say, and that when I had said them, I would wait for you to speak, and I thought that if you spoke to me as I had spoken to you, I would be grateful and go away."

"That dress looks good on you."

"I thought that if you spoke in any other way, it would show that you were making the mistake of thinking that *I* was all talk and no hands."

"It'd look better on a chair-back."

"I thought that I did not want you to make that mistake because I knew that it was a mistake you would die from."

"It'd look best in a circle on the floor."

The woman turned, and Bishop, his legs apart and

his thumbs hooked on his belt, was leaning against the door like an enormous pair of shears.

"You are a white son-of-a-bitch," she said, speaking not only to the man, but also to the entire contents of the room: to the furniture, to the cistern, to the chipped crockery, to the wall-paper patterns fading under a down of carbon, to wood and iron and glass and tin, to a bottle of arnica and a can of coal-oil, to soap. "You are a white son-of-a-bitch."

"Come upstairs nice."

"Not if God Himself pimped for you!"

"Come upstairs and take off that dress," Bishop said, "or I'll shuck you out of it like an ear of corn!"

"I don't like your smell," the woman said, and the words were words from the composite memory and the accrued hatred of her race. "I don't like your smell, white man."

Bishop's fist opened a vertical split across her lips, and blood ran at once from the bulging plus-sign of her mouth. "Now you're going to do it right here on the floor," he said.

There was no more speech, spoken but unheard; there was only motion, mute but eloquent—motion not from one alone toward the other, but from each toward each: there were two simultaneous bare-handed head-on attacks. The woman went for Bishop with the full arsenal of her body: she went for him with teeth, knees, knuckles, and nails; she went for him with breath, hair, bone, and brain—she went for him as if she were an act of nature occurring for his particular ruin, as if she were fire, pestilence, flood, famine, and death compounded and made personal. Bishop went for the woman with the rigid single purpose of a finger going for a ring, and it was as if for one time the part included the whole, as if the man himself had been drawn into his own locomotive erection.

Using his arms like a sprinter, Bishop coked the woman numb with a pair of lunges, and she fell as a book falls: a splay of pages splashing on the floor, stirring a little, and soon lying still. Clawing his fly, Bishop dove at her—wide open on the sand and splinters near the hot black squat of the stove, among the chain-gangs of grease-ants, the zig-zags of startled roaches, and the blurring polka-dots of her own blood—and there on the floor, feeling for an entrance like a bull, he sent his horn into her groin and gored her.

✿

### AT BIGELOW VROOM'S

*Deployed in a hollow square at the edge of the high square throat, a line of cross-stitches sprawled like riflemen,* but the square had been broken, and the riflemen were dead. *The sleeves fell full to overhang the cuffs, and on the cuffs too pickets of crosses lay prone* under scabs of crushed vermin. *Pleated at the neck-line and pleated at the waist, the loose and blooming blouse was blank yellow muslin,* blank once, but printed now with exclamation-points of blood. *From the waist, the skirt swept like a sweeping broom, and here and there, as if spun up from the floor, a solitary cross tumbled among the folds,* torn, greasy, soot-smeared, and rank. . . .

Staring at the staring woman, Vroom rose very slowly and went toward her. He took her by the arms, gently at first, still staring, and then tightly, as if to extravasate words from her eyes—and as if the words had loomed there and burst across the gap between meaning and understanding, he reached for the door of a cupboard: on the middle shelf, in a nest of silk rags, lay the Colt .38.

The woman picked up the gun and, saying nothing, started for the hallway.

"It'll shoot eight times," Vroom said.

✿

### PATTERN NUMBER 526 (cont'd.)

As before, Bishop was seated at the kitchen table, but he was naked now, and near his feet were a basin of faintly pink water, a damp towel, and a cake of laundry soap. A great fungus of smoke grew above him from a banded cigar, and it shrank—and in panic, ran—as the woman sent the door in.

"It'll shoot eight times," she said.

*The first shot would enter Bishop's left eye, and coming out with a mulligan of brain and broken bone, it would drill through a stove-plate and die among the embers and the ash. The second shot would core the skull from ear to ear, and the corpse would topple, the*

211

*head bouncing once, like an apple. The third shot would crack the spine and sing off it at an angle to slug a hole in a pot and drop, spent, into a marsh of hominy. The fourth shot, fired with both hands from both knees, would hit a pelvic hollow and flip the body half over, and the fifth, sixth, and seventh shots would geld it. The eighth shot. . . .*

"You'd better save the last one for yourself," Bishop said.

*Flies would come skiing down slopes of smoke to bring up short at blood, and roaches, in the silent room, would pause to paw the air. The woman, still kneeling, would turn the gun upon herself and long look at her handful of power and steel judgment, long look before a smile broke her broken face, and then she would kiss the gun on the mouth and turn it back upon Bishop. The eighth shot. . . .*

When the gun-sight was lowered from Bishop's left eye, that left eye was still a living part of a living one hundred and seventy pounds, and the blood of that body still passed into and out of its heart like a throng in a revolving-door. The eight shots—one in the barrel and seven in the magazine—remained unfired, and smoke still unwound from the coal and the now burning band of a cigar.

Bishop spoke to a vacant rectangle of night in the kitchen wall. "*I* ain't running," he said.

✿

Facing the zinc apron of a stove, Grace Paulhan sat in a parlor armchair that sat with its fat elbows on its fat knees. The stove was cold now, and the dull gray iron of its cheeks caught only a silver blear from a turned-down lamp. An alarm-clock on the mantel was surrendering at five minutes to one.

Shoes sandpapered the porch steps, and Platt came in, rattling the four panes of the door in their putty cross. "He wasn't there, the muzzler," he said, and he sailed his hat into a corner. "If he had of been, I'd of beat his brains out the back way—so help me God, I would!"

Grace leaned forward and spread her hands before the dead stove, as if the gesture without the fire would warm them. "I'm glad you didn't find him," she said.

"Christ, you talk like Dan Hunter!"

"That's not why I'm glad, Aaron."

"Dan and his little damn Bible!"

"The woman didn't want you to go."

"She ain't the only one has a say."

"What happened happened to *her*."

"Suppose next time it happens to you."

"Then the say'll be mine."

"And you wouldn't want me to do anything?" He picked up his hat and pushed out the dents. "You wouldn't want me to do anything, Gracie?"

She said nothing, looking down at the duck-feet of

the stove, at the flash-grain in the flooring, at a rag-rug with a maple-leaf pattern.

"You made the black woman lay down in your own room upstairs," he said, "a room that nobody in Warrensburg ever set his foot in, not even me. *You* can help her, but you don't want *me* to help her. You want to keep me out of your affairs, and the reason is the same old one you've had against me all along: what I done to Tom. What I done to Tom! I let a man die because he wasn't worth keeping alive, but, my God, Gracie, does that make me out as bad a man as Eli?"

She rose, turning away from him, and as she passed the lamp-table, she idled a finger through a faint fuzz of settled dust. "You don't understand, Aaron," she said.

"I ain't a smart one, Mrs. Paulhan."

"If you were, you'd have other ways of knowing things than being told."

"What would I know?"

"Why I don't want you to get in trouble."

"I ain't any smarter yet."

"This is Saturday night," she said, still turned away. "Except for one thing, it was going to be the same as every other Saturday night. You'd have come around about ten o'clock, the way you always do, and I'd have been sitting there in that chair waiting for you, the way I always am. When I heard you in the road, I'd have gone to the door, and it would be open before you started up the porch—you wouldn't have had to ring, Aaron; you never have to ring. And I'd have taken your hat and hung it up on the rack, and the two of us would've sat down and talked till we were tired of talking—an hour's worth, maybe, or only a word or two. And if you were hungry, I'd have gotten you something to eat—cake, pie, a cold-meat sandwich, tea, coffee, anything you wanted. And then if you didn't feel like smoking, you wouldn't have had to ask me to go into the bedroom; I'd have known without your telling me. . . . That would've been Saturday night, Aaron, that would've been tonight—except for one thing."

"Please say it, Gracie."

"Tonight," she said, "tonight when we were in bed I was going to say, 'Aaron, don't come here with money any more.' "

"You would of said that? If the woman hadn't of been here, you'd of said that, Gracie?"

A squall of pebbles struck the clapboards and clacked across the porch. Platt opened the door and peered into the dark. "Who's there?" he said.

"None of your business, Mister," a voice said.

"You night-crawling bastard!" Platt said, and he made for the steps.

"Come any further," the voice said, "and you're all done whooring." Steel slid on steel as a lever-action slotted home a cartridge. "Go back to bed, Mister. It's Saturday night."

✿

Streaks and points of light were showing on the dark blue glaze of the shade as Hunter raised it on a slate dawn. The world in the window-frame was an emulsion, and he saw mist-hung objects—trees, rocks, grass, hills—as if he were looking at them through an emptied milk-bottle.

Slocum's head wobbled, and opening his eyes, he moved lips and tongue to taste away the sour saliva of a three-hour nap. He cupped a hand close to the old man's mouth, and once more he brought out his watch and timed the pulse.

"Fifty-five," he said, looking up quickly at Hunter and then wondering down again to the old man. "I'll be God damned! Fifty-five, and even!"

Little Johnny Littlejohn stiffened slightly and broke wind. "What time is it?" he said.

"Time to get dressed for your funeral," Slocum said.

The old man squinted at Slocum's watch. "Close onto six. That's what I figured."

"How long've you been laying there *figuring*?"

"Damn near an hour."

"You're supposed to be dead as an ice-bag."

"You know what else I was figuring?" the old man said. "I was figuring if I first had a glass of hot milk, I'd be ready to eat me a breakfast."

"You want to know something, Daddy?" Slocum said. "You're just an old son-of-a-bitch."

"Watch out, bub. You're making small of my old lady."

"Your old lady's been dead eighty years, not including last night—and I swear to God that was another eighty years."

"Just for that," the old man said, "I'm going to shoot for a hundred and five—a hundred and five, bub. Before I'm done, I'm going to plague the almighty wishbone out of you."

Slocum put his hands on the old man's cheeks, saying, "Daddy, can I kiss you before I go home and order you some calendars?"

✿

## COMING INTO WARRENSBURG

Under the bridge near Thurman Station, the Hudson River cuts a deep groove in the sandy bottom, and here, at the fringe of the run, bass lie staring into its bottle-green gloom. In the eddies, the eight-oared shells of crawfish whirl, and now and then a frog drifts down, swimming a vain but endless breast-stroke against the current, and no other moving thing, alive or dead, rides the flow unseen by the kingfisher on the iron sling of the trestle, not the capsized moth, nor the beetle hugging a sponge of foam, nor even the drowning worm that tumbles end-over-end like phlegm. The morning is Sunday-silent, and no wind preens a forest of maples broken only by the river and the river-road. No hawk veers overhead, churning the risen churns of mist, and no animal—no spurting squirrel or chipmunk at prayer

—rustles the paper of outworn leaves. An asphalt mile is void, and over its mirages of oil the warming air begins to shimmer.

✿

## SERVICES FOR SUNDAY

The sun was an hour high when Slocum and Hunter approached the bridge on their way back from the Poor Home.

"Coming to church, Doc?"

"Without coffee, God gives me the shakes."

"I'll make you some strong enough to iron a shirt on."

"I like it so hard it stands up without a cup."

"You'll get it. If a man can *drink* coffee, it's weak."

As their feet struck the corduroy planking, a kingfisher dumped itself down for a catch and came out so low that its rush shirred the surface of the water; banking like a bat, with a steep right and left swerve, the bird pulled up flapping, and then, lance first, again it plunged.

Slocum saw no part of this foray, neither the bird, nor the strike, nor the capture of the minnow. He had been watching a twist of smoke untwist against a knoll at the far side of the river, and when he was certain that it rose from the hollow holding Number Four Pond, he touched Hunter's arm, his eyes shunting an unspoken query up the long converge of the bridge.

The timbers bustled as Hunter broke into a dead run for the bridgehead. The grains of sand between the sleepers came to life, simmering over each other like ants, and suddenly, when the running feet ran off onto the pavement, they died again. Quitting the road for an overgrown path, Hunter flogged his way into a catch-as-catch-can of underbrush that grappled him with every branch, twig, and leaf. They flailed him from face to foot; they whipped his throat, clutched his armpits, and invaded his crotch; and then, when he had passed on, they bushwhacked him from behind. Near the shoulder of the hollow he was fungoed to his knees, and on his knees he crawled into the clear around the pond sink.

Motionless in a saucer of sky, a small white church should have floated bottom-side up—a small bright box of a building, a belfried cube, a house of blocks and prisms put together by a child—but the church was gone, body, belfry, porch, and all, and floating in its place, and bottom-side up, was a rubble of ash, brick, and plaster. A few clinkers were still alive, sending down a rope of smoke for ripples to unravel.

Slowly Hunter descended to the rim of the pond, and slowly, always with his eyes in the ring drawn around itself by the fire, he walked toward it, his feet lightly dusted off by little besoms of volunteer wheat worked by the occasional wind. Entering upon the gravel strip leading to the vanished flight of steps, he stopped. Three people were waiting for him: Aaron Platt, Grace Paulhan, and America Smith, the last wearing a borrowed dress and carrying her stained own over her arm.

In Warrensburg, one mile down the Schroon River fork, a dog barked four times, the sound skimming the water like the shadow of a cloud. It was spread thin by the time it galloped up the hill to the hollow, and America Smith spoke only when it had passed and run away.

"Eli Bishop," she said.

The two words sank to the floor of Hunter's stomach and grew cold, like submarine stones. He tried to look the woman in the face, but the ceiling of the world he stood in was too low, and, cramped, he could raise his eyes no higher than her shoulders: he could see a headless body flanked by a pair of hydrangeas that had been burned at the stake; he could see the spikes of the iron fence, torn up to writhe like a dynamited right-of-way; he could see the church-bell, thrown clear like a hat in an accident, lying among a few blistered cans of kerosene. He could see, too, the privy among the lilacs, and he wept for the first time when he saw that the cabinet had been pulled away, that on the hill of dung and paper stood his pulpit, equipped as always with pitcher, glass, and Bible, but labelled now with a single word drawn in coal. The word was "MEN."

"Eli Bishop," the woman said.

Kicking aside the kerosene tins, Hunter dragged the fallen bell to the burial-ground and slung it by its yoke between two stones standing back to back. He took up the stump of the clapper-rope and jerked it once, as if it were the lanyard of a piece of artillery: a corrugated bronze bash lumbered off into the woods, ricocheting from tree to tree until it was lost.

"No princes of the wilderness of Sinai," he said, and he talked as if to peopled benches in a church still standing, "no princes are those that come now with gifts before the Lord: no Nahshon and Nethaneel with a silver charger full of a fine flour mingled with oil, *but Emerson Polhemus and Sam Pirie with brass*; no Eliab and Elizur with a silver bowl, *but Joel Confrey and Edom Smead with hatred*; no Shelumiel and Eliasaph with a golden spoon of incense, *but Herbert Estes and Leland Polk with greed*; no Elishama and Gamaliel with a young bullock, *but Ash Harned and Mark Lomax with wrath*; no Abidan and Ahiezer with a first-year lamb, *but Arthur Hustis and Abel French with vanity*; no Pagiel and Ahira with a kid of the goats, *but Jerome Piper with coal-oil and lust, and Eli Bishop with Death!* . . . . Eli Bishop! Eli Bishop!"

He tried, as if the name were a poison taken by mistake, to spit it away, to disgorge it, but even with the muscles of his belly making a fist, they tightened only as a hand tightens on sand, and the poison eluded him and was gone.

"Eli Bishop!" he said. "Eli Bishop!"

The man's face cropped up everywhere, surrounding Hunter like the stencilled repetitions of a wall-paper design: it covered the gravestones, and the granite cherubs wore it, and the granite urns; it flew with the flies, and among the trembling trees it did a jack-o'-lantern jig; it turned with each milling flake of dust, and like a tinsel target, it bobbed on the fountain of smoke.

"Eli Bishop!"

And now, as Hunter made the bell flare into a sun-burst of sound, he cried out into the metal bedlam, say-ing, "Dwellers in the dirt, I call you from the hollow of your mattress and the bulge of your hammock, I call you from pancakes and long sweetening, I call you from neighbors' fences and neighbors' wives! Forget the swing of their skirts and the smell of their hair, forget the claims you jump only at night, forget the greener grass you sprawl on in spring dreams! And you that swing the skirts, come in wire and whalebone, o mothers of a mighty race, come with paper cherries dangling from your hats and linen leaves! Come in starch and faint camphor, o lady pioneers, come in vici-kid and black cotton hose! Come on heels of rubber, o you daughters of Virginia Dare, come, and come you mum-bling with rubber gums! Come one, come all you that have washed your hands in innocency and overlooked the blood on your sleeves! Unspotted lambs of the Lord, come you walking righteously from the haymow of the world to the haymow of Heaven, come you with straw on your knees and straw on the backs of your camisoles! Come, brother sons-of-bitches, come one, come all!"

✿

Funneled in elms, the road through Warrensburg was empty and quiet—empty except for a scratching dog, and quiet except for the undulant anger of a mile-away bell. No rockers creaked behind the grape-vines, no covey of voices whirred up from the grass, and in the houses the muffled clatter of morning had reached a void.

The dog stopped scratching and yawned, and at the peak of the yawn a squeak emerged. There was motion now along the edges of the highway, slow-motion, and there was small sound—the dry gargle of dry spokes, the lisp of shoes in sand, the rumor of whispered questions—and starting at the vanishing-point of the road, a procession gathered numbers as it went along and finally turned the village inside-out, like the finger of a glove.

Warrensburg came in ones, twos, threes, and rambling droves: it came in britches, overalls, and picnic gingham; it came egg-bald, bearded, and framed in down; it came with truss, corset, crutch, and slingshot; it came from bed, barn, stove, and posture in the shade; it came gray, auburn, blue-black, and blond; it came with goiter, asthma, epilepsy, and invincibility to all illness but the last; it came hard-shell, Friend, papist, and Abenaki; it came wife, mother, daughter, and spinster sister; it came husband, father, son, and whoremonger.

✵

A chipmunk ran a scallop over a crumbling tomb, a ruby hummer played among the thistles like a spark, and a wind, prying, left fingerprints on the window of the pond. From the pulpit in the lilacs, Hunter glanced east over faces at a full-rigged cloud bowling hull-down toward Maine.

"I preach to you, I crow from this dung-hill, for the last time," he said, and turning back the cover of the Bible, he felt his eyes being picked at by the words *To The Most High And Mighty Prince JAMES, By The Grace Of God KING . . .*, and then he looked up, covering the dedication-page with his hand. "In the First Book of Moses, called Genesis, God spoke, saying, 'I will make man in my image and after my likeness, and I will give him dominion over the fish of the sea, and over the fowl of the air, and over the cattle, and over all the earth, and over every creeping thing that creepeth upon the earth, and I will bless him and say unto him: Be fruitful, and multiply, and replenish the earth, and subdue it.' And so speaking, God made man, and, behold, man had been made in the image of God and after His likeness, and God was pleased, and the evening and the morning were the sixth day.

"It is now the seventh day," Hunter said, and his hand came away from the Bible a fist clutching an india-paper sheaf, "it is now the seventh and the sanctified day, and on this seventh day I say before God that if truly He made us in His own image, then truly in worshipping Him we worship ourselves: we are either Gods blessing a God, or men blessing a man, or many dogs bowing down before the King of the Beasts, but whether it be one or another, our admiration and adoring are performed for a mirror, and always will we see out of our eyes only our eyes seeing in."

224

He threw the pages away, and for a moment he watched them lurch and sidle down the air. "Being that which sees and that which is seen," he said, "being one of many that are all the same, each of us will eat till, eating, he vomits; each will scratch without end; each will lift his leg to every rock in a world of rocks; and each, each will rise from his sweating slumber to lope miles and miles after the heat that cooked his dreams. We will root and itch and sleep and rut, but if God is a dog, then we will not blame ourselves for being dogs, for dogs will do these things. Nor will we blame ourselves for pulling down the tabernacle, for if God is a God, then we too are Gods, and surely God will bring such a church as ours into the dust. And finally, if God is a man, then all of us are men, and we will not assail men for being what they are: only in private will we stone a dog, but not ever nor anywhere will we stone a looking-glass. We will judge not, only that we be not judged, for we are all guilty, *all*, and we will overlook the black heart in others because we know that we also are afflicted with heart-disease. We will accept our loud greed, and we will not be astounded at the bones we break with words. We will be right by day and wrong by night, we will lie and be lied to, we will be generous for six per cent, and we will turn the other cheek only to hunt for a brick. Being people, we will do these things, for people, as one of our more public whores once said, people ain't such a much."

They heard him: mounted on the rounder stones, upright in the grass aisles, squatting on their boot-heels, shoring up their wagons, straddling the limbs of trees, stiff-legged, cross-legged, spread-legged, sitting, standing, lying down, and leaning: they heard him.

"Being people made in the image of God, or being Gods made after the likeness of dogs, we will root and itch and sleep and rut: we will hole up in a haystack when not even our hair can stand on end, and thenceforward, from baldness to baldness, from early in the morning till late in the afternoon, we will lust to be chambering, and we will find provision for the flesh though we must seek it in the hollow of our hand, though we must pay money for it or marry it. . . ."

And now he looked upon the face that he had been speaking to by speaking to all the other faces—Eli Bishop's—and as he watched, as the others too turned to watch, Bishop stopped one of his nostrils with a thumb and fired an acrobat of mucus over a nearby grave.

". . . We will find it," Hunter said, "in the end, we will find it though we must take it by force."

"If you're talking about anybody special," Bishop said, "name names."

"I name God for creating you."

"I was created by a old cock name of Waldo Bishop."

"And I name you for destroying America Smith."

Bishop rose from a crouch, dropping a few pebbles and dusting his hands. He looked at the woman, saying, "What else is a nigger for?"

There were eyes now unable to remain on Bishop's face. Mansfield, white-goods Henry Mansfield, picked at the rotting pastry of a brownstone marker; Doc Slocum cinched a loose button on his coat; Aaron Platt bathed his vision in the water-color distance; Grace Paulhan, standing next to America Smith, took up a black hand and smoothed and smoothed the fingers; and Trubee Pell, and Bigelow Vroom, and Dolly Piper, and Pearl Hustis, and Tombigbee Quinn, and Helen Smead, and Gus Ritchie, and Dave Updegrove, and Cleo and Jeff Branch, and Lizzie Cass, and Abe Novinsky, and Clara Penrose—all these too withdrew.

"I'm asking what else is a nigger for?"

Bishop made his way to the pulpit, where Hunter, saying nothing, stood staring down at his torn Bible. "You told me once that you wasn't a preacher all the time," he said. "You told me that you was a man too, eating, snoring, taking a snootful, and shaving, just like all the rest of us. . . . Well, Mister Christer, you was bragging. As a man, you're such a damn bag of wind that if it wasn't for a tight collar, you could stay in your clothes while they got pressed. When you ain't preaching, you don't sound more than half-proud—*so preach, Mister Christer: it's Sunday!*"

Hunter's tears were glass eyes, and the Bible flickered under them as he turned the pages to the place-ribbon, now lying in Deuteronomy. "I will read to you now," he said, "from the Fifth Book of Moses, chapter 22, verses 28 and 29. . . . 'If a man find a damsel that is a virgin, which is not betrothed, and lay hold on her, and lie with her, and they be found, then the man that

227

lay with her shall give unto the damsel's father fifty shekels of silver, and she shall be his wife. . . .' "

He looked at the words as if they had spoken of themselves, as if he were hearing them announce for the first time the meaning of their rigid combinations, and suddenly his face shrank, and he spat down at the book. "She shall be his wife!" he said, and he shoved the Bible over the edge of the pulpit to fall with a crumpled-paper crash into the stoneboat. "She shall be his wife, the Good Book says, she shall be his wife though of all things on earth that live—of all things that walk, crawl, fly, swim, dig, or hop—she holds him least! And he, he shall wipe out his sin with fifty pieces of silver, only twenty more than Judas took to betray Christ! This shall be his fine for the misdemeanor of rape—a stack of coins, a half-filled dime-bank—but it is not enough, I say, it is not enough . . . !"

A long-slung clench of lightly-padded bone, a stone in the snowball of Bishop's fist, hit Hunter flush on the mouth, on the nose, and again on the mouth, and blood was flung like drops of water by a wet dog. Hunter covered his face with his hands, but they leaked, and he took them away just as Bishop pitched a roundhouse against a back corner of his lower jaw: his head struck the ground before his feet did.

Bishop turned now upon the congregation. "Who else thinks a white man marrying a nigger ain't enough?" he said, and looking from face to face, he walked among them. "Who else thinks a white man marrying a nigger flipping-jinny ain't enough?"

228

It was enough for an old man pulling again and again at the hair in his ears, Emerson Polhemus, and it was enough for Leland Polk, who was carefully honing a pen-knife on a stone. It was enough too for Sam Pirie, who was cracking his finger-joints, and Joel Confrey, who was chewing a twig. It was enough for Herb Estes the undertaker, for Ed Smead the sheriff, for Ash Harned the post-master. It was enough for Jerome Piper and his taped-up son Marvin, for plain Miss Finch, and for Mark Lomax the believer in Jesus Christ. It was enough for all these and enough for others, for Art Hustis, Abel French, Hannah Harned, and Sarah Ritchie.

"Who else thinks a white man marrying a nigger hump ain't enough?"

"Me."

Faces spun to face the origin of the voice.

"Me," Bigelow Vroom said. "*Me!*"

"Take off your coat, Indian!" Bishop said.

"You'd steal it, pale-face," Vroom said.

And they closed, and from the start, from four hundred years before the start, both fought to kill: four hundred years of plundering and systematic murder to retain were fighting four hundred years of retreat and headlong dying to repossess. For Bishop, the scoured surface was clean; for Vroom, the stain of history had penetrated to the last drop of water that could be distilled from his blood or wrung from his bone: in the one slept memories of the creeping barrage of his race, the transcontinental night of the white man's coming; in the other, the memories lay awake.

The fight was short. The two men stood a foot apart, their arms reciprocating like the pistons of a single engine, their bodies sending and receiving until their clothes were the flapping remnants of a man sucked into running machinery—and then the machine, choked, began to shake itself to pieces. It tore loose from its base, and, racing now, it flowed vibrant away. Vroom fell only when his hands were in boxing-gloves of morphine, only when his shocked face seemed to be held together by the capillary continuity of his blood.

Bishop wheeled on the crowd and stood poised, but only a killdeer, on the wing, broke the silence with its two-word fiat. "An hour after he can walk," he said, nodding back at Vroom, "we're going to have a parade in this town, and he's going to head it." He stooped to pick up a pine-cone. "It'll start at the Post Office, and it'll keep on moving till it's out of sight. There'll be four people marching in that parade: this Indian here, the Indian's boy-bastard Aben, the nigger-woman, and one more." He cracked a few scales from the cone and let them fall. "The Jew." He looked now at Novinsky. "The Jew son-of-a-bitch: he goes too. This use to be a white man's town, Warrensburg, and it won't be long before it's white all over again." A butterfly beat past, its speckled wings applauding.

America Smith was a grave-length away, her hands, as if in a muff, hidden by the drape of the spare dress. She brought one of them forth, and the black accusa-

230

tion of the Colt was leveled at Bishop. "Run," she said.

"Put that gun down, nigger!"

"Now pray and run."

"Did you hear me, nig . . . !"

A bullet stopped Bishop's last syllable at his teeth, and teeth tumbled from a second mouth that opened in the back of his head. A dead man did a half-twist, gave at the joints, and collapsed.

Still holding the Colt, the woman polled the faces of the crowd, remembering: ". . . *I looked always for the white face that would say, even only with its eyes, 'My hand is not raised against you,'* " and then saying, "And now there are many faces!"

✿

She tossed the gun into neutral ground, and it rode roughly on its side to stop near the feet of Sheriff Smead. He was looking downward when it slid through the cone of his vision, but he did not follow it, nor did he notice the dust on his shoes or, on one of the toe-caps, a mold of ash flourishing in a culture of kerosene: the gun, the ground, the sunlit facets of glassy gravel, these and all other things were vague fill-in around the only fact in focus—a line of cross-stitch encircling a sleeve.

He went toward the woman, avoiding the gun and avoiding too a worn-out and unmarked little mound, and he put his hand on the torn dress, saying, as he ran a finger over the brown and green and dry-blood embroidery, "I'm sorry it got spoiled. I thought it was

231

kind of nice." And now he looked up at the woman. "I'm glad about something else, though. I'm glad you found out Dan was wrong about people: they *are* such a much, ma'am."

He turned away, and passing through the crowd to take the path along the pond-bank, he did not pause once, nor did he once glance back, before disappearing over the crown of the hill.

✿

*Toluca Lake, California*
*May 31, 1943*

JOHN SANFORD was born in the Harlem section of New York City in 1904 and attended public schools there. He graduated from Lafayette College and finally Fordham University, where he earned a degree in law. He was admitted to the bar in 1929 and at about that time, influenced by his friend Nathanael West, began to write. Among his twentysome books are eight novels, of which his favorites are *A Man without Shoes, Seventy Times Seven, The Land That Touches Mine,* and *The People from Heaven.*

ALAN WALD, Professor of English Literature and American Culture at the University of Michigan, is the author of *James T. Farrell* (1978), *The Revolutionary Imagination* (1983), *The New York Intellectuals* (1987), *The Responsibility of Intellectuals* (1992), and *Writing from the Left* (1994).